J. G. BALLARD was born in 1930 in Shanghai. After internment in a civilian prison camp, his family returned to England after World War II. His 1984 bestseller *Empire of the Sun* won the Guardian Fiction Prize and the James Tait Black Memorial Prize. His controversial novel *Crash* was made into a film by David Cronenberg. His autobiography *Miracles of Life* was published in 2008, and a collection of interviews with the author, *Extreme Metaphors*, was published in 2012. J. G. Ballard passed away in 2009.

also by j. g. ballard

concrete
island

concrete island

(a novel)

j. g. ballard

picador | farrar, straus & giroux | new york

CONCRETE ISLAND. Copyright © 1973 by J. G. Ballard. Introduction copyright © 2014 by Neil Gaiman. All rights reserved. Printed in the United States of America. For information, address Picador, 175 Fifth Avenue, New York, N.Y. 10010.

picadorusa.com • instagram.com/picador
twitter.com/picadorusa • facebook.com/picador

Picador® is a U.S. registered trademark and is used by Macmillan Publishing Group, LLC, under license from Pan Books Limited.

For book club information, please visit facebook.com/picadorbookclub or email marketing@picadorusa.com.

Designed by Devan Norman

The Library of Congress has cataloged the Farrar, Straus and Giroux edition as follows:

Names: Ballard, J. G., 1930–2009.
Title: Concrete Island. / J. G. Ballard.
Description: New York: Farrar, Straus and Giroux, 1974, c1973.
Identifiers: LCCN 73087699 | ISBN 9780374128074 (hardcover)
Subjects: Science fiction.
Classification: LCC PZ4.B1893 Co3 PR6052.A46 | DDC 823'.9'14—dc23
LC record available at https://lccn.loc.gov/73087699

Second Picador Paperback ISBN 978-1-250-17152-8

Our books may be purchased in bulk for promotional, educational, or business use. Please contact your local bookseller or the Macmillan Corporate and Premium Sales Department at 1-800-221-7945, extension 5442, or by email at MacmillanSpecialMarkets@macmillan.com.

First published by Farrar, Straus and Giroux

First Picador Paperback Edition: October 2001
Second Picador Paperback Edition: June 2018

D   11

contents

the concrete insulation

by neil gaiman

Memories of J. G. Ballard, Jim to his friends—and I was never one of them, I was too young when I arrived in the world of writers, and too new, but still, he's Jim Ballard, which was how I was introduced to him, like the boy in *Empire of the Sun*. He was standing beside William Burroughs at an art opening, affable and dry and avuncular, in a suburban way, as he observed the 80s artistic freakshow that surrounded him and somehow managed at the same time to be both part of it and not. I did not talk to him, then or any of the times I could have done. I was awed, and he always seemed too near and too far away.

Children, the kind who read, read everything that they find in the house; they read their parents' books (the ones the parents had as children, the ones they had as adults); they read Daniel Defoe's *Robinson Crusoe* alongside Isaac Asimov's *Caves of Steel*; *Coral Island* then *Dune Messiah*; *The Island of Adventure* beside *Conan the Adventurer*: they read all the books they can because they are there, and because they offer information and escape. Or I did, anyway.

Also, I knew we were all headed for the future, and I wanted to know what things would be like there, surrounded by robots, with our hand-held communications devices.

Which meant that, growing up, two of my favourite books were *The Crystal World* by J. G. Ballard, a strange apocalypse I barely understood, and to which I was attracted by the cover, showing a beautiful, glassy landscape, and the back cover blurb, telling me that this about people exploring the Amazonian rainforest, trying to find out why the world was becoming crystal, and *SF 12* edited by Judith Merrill, the book in which I discovered R.A. Lafferty and William Burroughs, Samuel R. Delany and Kit Reed, Carol Emshwiller and Fritz Leiber, Brian Aldiss and Tuli Kupferberg and a host of authors and ideas, including a story called "The Cloud Sculpters of Coral D", by J. G. Ballard, about a cloud sculpture and the men who fly small planes, about love and about murder.

These books meant that Ballard was, in my head, part of the club of SF writers, the people who wrote things I loved even if I did not entirely understand them, and this meant I read everything by him that I could find. And, when, aged 13 I changed schools, I discovered a school library filled with books that had not been in my previous school library: I found Mervyn Peake's *Gormenghast* books there, and *The Master and Margerita* and *1984* (which I read mostly to understand Bowie's *Diamond Dogs* and because there were jokes in the Alan Coren *1984* parody in *Punch* I suspected I was missing), and, on a high shelf, a tiny clutch of Ballard novels.

I read *Crash* first. I did not understand it, but I loved the writing, loved the smell of leather upholstery and the jewelled glitter of broken glass on the motorway. It seemed peculiarly intellectual: Elizabeth Taylor and crashing cars for sexual pleasure were both very abstract concepts for a teenager who had not been a teenager for very long.

Then I read *Concrete Island*, and I was in love.

I did not read then for character or for language (although I could be hooked by either and responded to both); I read for STORY, and in *Concrete Island*, I recognised a story, and came upon a story I recognised. It was Robinson Crusoe: here was a man, Robert Maitland, stranded on an island, cut off from civilisation, learning how to feed himself and to survive, always obsessed by the need to get off the island, get back to civilisation, to his wife, to his company, to his mistress, to his world.

I was of an age where I could start to see metaphor and pattern. *He's on an island*, I thought, *and he's been on an island his whole life.* It was a revelation.

I thrilled, reading it then, as I thrilled each time I re-read it since, to Maitland's problem-solving in the first few chapters: his plans to send up signal flares, his need for drinkable water, his attempts to get people to see him and stop. His joy at the thrown-away chips. Robinson Crusoe had breadfruit and other foodstuffs alien to a small boy in Sussex. He didn't have the chips that a lorry driver didn't want.

I was saddened and thrilled when Maitland found that he was not alone on his island: Crusoe had Friday, had that footprint in the sand. Maitland had two people, adults I barely understood, whose behaviour to him seemed pretty much right: I was a schoolboy, after all, and casual cruelty was usual. *Lord of the Flies* and *Unman, Wittering and Zigo* both seemed, to my eyes, to be realistic fiction about the way the children around me behaved, or would behave given half a chance.

* * *

Reading *Concrete Island* now, I read it with adult eyes. And if you have not read the book, stop reading this introduction here. The story is too good to spoil for you, after all.

I marvel at Ballard's ability to bring the Coral Island home, to recognise that a traffic island was, for someone stranded upon it, as remote as the South Seas. I am fascinated by the politics of Friday, and the way that Ballard breaks that role in two, and subverts it, and how savage Maitland needs to become in order to gain dominion over his Island Kingdom. Friday, the savage that Crusoe rescues, who knows more of the island and the ways of survival than Crusoe ever will, becomes two survivors who use the island to represent their own escape from the world: a mentally subnormal acrobat, and a young woman whose own tragedies are never explained, only implied, and who leaves the island and returns, a heart-hurt whore who no longer fits the world she fled. Both people Maitland would look down on in everyday life, both people on whom he finds himself depending for his survival.

I admire the way the island is a palimpsest, that the world, the town, before the motorway existed shows through, just as Robinson Crusoe shows through in *Concrete Island*, from time to time.

I did not understand when I was a boy that the best way to prepare for the future I would find myself living in as an adult would be to read the work of J. G. Ballard. That the people who were offering me generation starships and galactic empires were a distraction: that it was Ballard who was writing the world I would grow into. I don't think I understood that until the crash-death of Princess Diana, and I knew that I had been here before, and in whose pages.

Concrete Island is an artefact of its time, but one could write something very similar now. One would need to deal with the mobile phone issue—probably destroyed in the initial crash—but I wonder how many of us would actually stop, or let anybody know, if we saw the filthy man in the motorway island, and how many of us are able to escape the islands we now find ourselves marooned upon.

concrete
island

1

through the crash barrier

Soon after three o'clock on the afternoon of April 22nd 1973, a 35-year-old architect named Robert Maitland was driving down the high-speed exit lane of the Westway interchange in central London. Six hundred yards from the junction with the newly built spur of the M4 motorway, when the Jaguar had already passed the 70 m.p.h. speed limit, a blowout collapsed the front nearside tyre. The exploding air reflected from the concrete parapet seemed to detonate inside Robert Maitland's skull. During the few seconds before his crash he clutched at the whiplashing spokes of the steering wheel, dazed by the impact of the chromium window pillar against his head. The car veered from side to side across the empty traffic lanes, jerking his hands like a puppet's. The shredding tyre laid a black diagonal stroke across the white marker lines that followed the long curve of the motorway embankment. Out of control, the car burst through the palisade of pinewood trestles that formed a temporary barrier along the edge of the road. Leaving the hard shoulder, the car plunged down the grass slope of the embankment. Thirty yards ahead, it came to a halt against the rusting chassis of an overturned taxi. Barely injured by this violent tangent that had grazed his life, Robert Maitland lay across his steering wheel, his jacket and trousers studded with windshield fragments like a suit of lights.

In these first minutes as he recovered, Robert Maitland could remember little more of the crash than the sound of the exploding tyre, the swerving sunlight as the car emerged from the tunnel of an overpass, and the shattered windshield stinging his face. The sequence of violent events only microseconds in duration had opened and closed behind him like a vent of hell.

'... my God ...'

Maitland listened to himself, recognizing the faint whisper. His hands still rested on the cracked spokes of the steering wheel, fingers splayed out nervelessly as if they had been dissected. He pressed his palms against the rim of the wheel, and pushed himself upright. The car had come to rest on sloping ground, surrounded by nettles and wild grass that grew waist-high outside the windows.

Steam hissed and spurted from the crushed radiator of the car, spitting out drops of rusty water. A hollow roaring sounded from the engine, a mechanical death rattle.

Maitland stared into the steering well below the instrument panel, aware of the awkward posture of his legs. His feet lay among the pedals as if they had been hurriedly propped there by the mysterious demolition squad which had arranged the accident.

He moved his legs, reassured as they took up their usual position on either side of the steering column. The pedal pressure responded to the balls of his feet. Maitland ignored the grass and the motorway outside and began a careful inventory of his body.

He tested his thighs and abdomen, brushed the fragments of windshield glass from his jacket and pressed his rib cage, exploring the bones for any sign of fracture.

In the driving mirror he examined his head. A triangular bruise like the blade of a trowel marked his right temple. His forehead was covered with flecks of dirt and oil carried into the car by the breaking windshield. Maitland squeezed his face, trying to massage some expression into the pallid skin and musculature. His heavy jaw and hard cheeks were drained of all blood. The eyes staring back at him from the mirror were blank and unresponsive, as if he were looking at a psychotic twin brother.

Why had he driven so fast? He had left his office in Marylebone at three o'clock, intending to avoid the rush-hour traffic, and had ample time to cruise along in safety. He remembered swerving into the central drum of the Westway interchange, and pressing on towards the tunnel of the overpass. He could still hear the tyres as they beat along the concrete verge, boiling off a slipstream of dust and cigarette packets. As the car emerged from the vault of the tunnel the April sunlight had rainbowed across the windshield, momentarily blinding him . . .

His seat belt, rarely worn, hung from its pinion by his shoulder. As Maitland frankly recognized, he invariably drove well above the speed limit. Once inside a car some rogue gene, a strain of rashness, overran the rest of his usually cautious and clearminded character. Today, speeding along the motorway when he was already tired after a three-day conference, preoccupied by the slight duplicity involved in seeing his wife so soon after a week spent with Helen Fairfax, he had almost wilfully devised the crash, perhaps as some bizarre kind of rationalization.

Shaking his head at himself, Maitland knocked out the last of the windshield with his hand. In front of him was the rusting chassis of the overturned taxi into which the Jaguar had slammed. Half hidden by the nettles, several other wrecks lay nearby, stripped of their tyres and chromium trim, rusty doors leaning open.

Maitland stepped from the Jaguar and stood in the waist-high grass. As he steadied himself against the roof the hot cellulose stung his hand. Shielded by the high embankment, the still air was heated by the afternoon sun. A few cars moved along the motorway, their roofs visible above the balustrade. A line of deep ruts, like the incisions of a giant scalpel, had been scored by the Jaguar in the packed earth of the embankment, marking the point where he had left the road a hundred feet from the overpass tunnel. This section of the motorway and its slip roads to the west of the interchange had been opened to traffic only two months earlier, and lengths of the crash barrier had yet to be installed.

Maitland waded through the grass to the front of his car. A single glance told him that he had no hope of driving it to a nearby access road. The front end had been punched into itself like a collapsed face. Three of the four headlamps were broken, and the decorative grille was meshed into the radiator honeycomb. On impact the suspension units had forced the engine back off its mountings, twisting the frame of the car. The sharp smell of antifreeze and hot rust cut at Maitland's nostrils as he bent down and examined the wheel housing.

A total write-off—damn it, he had liked the car. He walked through the grass to a patch of clear ground between the Jaguar and the embankment. Surprisingly, no one had yet stopped to help him. As the drivers emerged from the darkness below the overpass into the fast right-hand bend lit by the afternoon sunlight they would be too busy to notice the scattered wooden trestles.

Maitland looked at his watch. It was three eighteen, little more than ten minutes since the crash. Walking about through the grass, he felt almost light-headed, like a man who has just witnessed some harrowing event, a motorway pileup or public execution . . . He had promised his eight-year-old son that he would be home in time to collect him from school. Maitland visualized David at that moment, waiting patiently outside the Richmond Park gates near the military hospital, unaware that his father was six miles away, stranded beside a crashed car at the foot of a motorway embankment. Ironically, in this warm spring weather the line of crippled war veterans would be sitting in their wheelchairs by the park gates, as if exhibiting to the boy the variety of injuries which his father might have suffered.

Maitland went back to the Jaguar, steering the coarse grass out of the way with his hands. Even this small exertion flushed his face and chest. He looked round for the last time, with the deliberate gaze of a man inspecting an unhappy terrain he is about to leave for ever. Still shaken by the crash, he was already aware of the bruises across his thighs and chest. The impact had hurled him like a broken punch-bag on to the steering wheel—the second collision, as safety engineers modestly termed it. Calming himself, he leaned against the Jaguar's trunk; he wanted to fix in his mind this place of wild grass and abandoned cars where he had very nearly lost his life.

Shielding his eyes from the sunlight, Maitland saw that he had crashed into a small traffic island, some two hundred yards long and triangular in shape, that lay in the waste ground between three converging motorway routes. The apex of the island pointed towards the west and the declining sun, whose warm light lay over the distant television studios at White City. The base was formed by the southbound overpass that swept past seventy feet above the ground. Supported on massive concrete pillars, its six lanes of traffic were sealed from view by the corrugated metal splash guards installed to protect the vehicles below.

Behind Maitland was the northern wall of the island, the thirty-feet-high embankment of the westbound motorway from which he had crashed. Facing him, and forming the southern boundary, was the steep embankment of the three-lane feeder road which looped in a north-westerly circuit below the overpass and joined the motorway at the apex of the island. Although no more than a hundred yards away, this freshly grassed slope seemed hidden behind the overheated light of the island, by the wild grass, abandoned cars and builder's equipment. Traffic moved along the westbound lanes of the feeder road, but the metal crash barriers screened the island from the drivers. The high masts of three route indicators rose from concrete caissons built into the shoulder of the road.

Maitland turned as an airline coach passed along the motorway. The passengers on the upper deck, bound for Zurich, Stuttgart and Stockholm, sat stiffly in their seats like a party of mannequins. Two of them, a middle-aged man in a white raincoat and a young Sikh wearing a turban on his small head, looked down at Maitland, catching his eyes for a few seconds. Maitland returned their gaze, deciding not to wave at them. What did they think he was doing there? From the upper deck of the bus his Jaguar might well appear to be undamaged, and they would assume that he was a highway official or traffic engineer.

Below the overpass, at the eastern end of the island, a wire-mesh fence sealed off the triangle of waste ground from the area beyond, which had become an unofficial municipal dump. In the shadows below the concrete span were several derelict furniture vans, a stack of stripped-down billboards, mounds of tyres and untreated metal refuse. A quarter of a mile to the east of the overpass, visible through the fence, was a neighbourhood shopping centre. A red double-decker bus circled a small square, passing the striped awnings of multiple stores.

Clearly there was no exit from the island other than the embankments. Maitland removed the ignition keys from the instrument panel and unlocked the Jaguar's trunk. The chances of a wandering tramp or tinker finding the car were slight—the island was sealed off from the world around it by the high embankments on two sides and the wire-mesh fence on its third. The compulsory landscaping had yet to be carried out by the contractors, and the original contents of this shabby tract, its rusting cars and coarse grass, were still untouched.

Holding the handle of his leather overnight case, Maitland tried to lift it from the trunk. He found himself fainting from the exertion. The blood had drained instantly from his head, as if the minimum circulation was being maintained. He put down the case and leaned weakly against the open lid of the trunk.

In the polished panels of the rear wheel housing Maitland stared at the distorted reflection of himself. His tall figure was warped like a grotesque scarecrow, and his white-skinned face bled away in the curving contours of the bodywork. A madman's grimace, one ear on a pedicle six inches from his head.

The crash had shaken him more than he realized. Maitland glanced down at the contents of the trunk—the tool kit, a clutter of architectural journals, and a cardboard crate holding half a dozen bottles of white Burgundy which he was taking home for his wife, Catherine. After the death of his grandfather the previous year Maitland's mother had been giving him some of the old man's wines.

'Maitland, you could use a drink now . . .' he told himself aloud. He locked the trunk, reached into the back of the car and picked up his raincoat, hat and briefcase. The crash had jerked loose a clutter of forgotten items from beneath the seats—a half-empty tube of sun lotion, memento of a holiday he had taken at La Grande Motte with Dr Helen Fairfax, the preprint of a paper she had given at a paediatric seminar, a packet of Catherine's miniature cigars he had hidden when trying to make her give up smoking.

Holding his briefcase in his left hand, hat on his head, raincoat over his right shoulder, Maitland set off towards the embankment. It was three thirty-one, still less than half an hour since the accident.

He looked back for the last time at the island. Already the waist-high grass, marked by the winding corridors that recorded his uncertain movements around the car, was settling itself again, almost hiding the silver Jaguar. A thin yellow light lay across the island, an unpleasant haze that seemed to rise from the grass, festering over the ground as if over a wound that had never healed.

A truck's diesel engine thundered below the overpass. Turning his back on the island, Maitland stepped on to the foot of the embankment and clambered up the soft slope. He would climb the embankment, wave down a passing car and be on his way.

2

the embankment

The earth flowed around him like a warm, alluvial river. Halfway up the embankment Maitland found himself sinking to his knees in the sliding slope. An unpacked topsoil intended only to carry the grass cover, the earth had not yet been consolidated by the seedlings sprouting through its open surface. Maitland laboured away, searching for a firm foothold and using the briefcase as a paddle. The effort of climbing the embankment had almost exhausted him, but he forced himself on.

Tasting blood in his mouth, he stopped and sat down. Squatting on the powdery slope, he took the handkerchief from his pocket and touched his tongue and lips. The red stain formed the imprint of his shaky mouth, like an illicit kiss. Maitland felt the tender skin of his right temple and cheekbone. The bruise ran from the ear as far as his right nostril. Pressing a finger into the nasal cleft, he could feel the injured sinus and gums, a loosened eyetooth.

Waiting for his breath to return, Maitland listened to the traffic moving above his head. The sound of engines drummed

ceaselessly through the tunnel of the overpass. On the far side of
the island the feeder road was busy now, and Maitland waved his
raincoat at the passing cars. However, the drivers were concentrating on the overhead route indicators and the major junction with
the motorway.

The towers of the distant office blocks rose into the afternoon
air. Searching the warm haze over Marylebone, Maitland could
almost identify his own building. Somewhere behind the glass
curtain wall on the seventeenth floor his secretary was typing the
agenda for the following week's finance committee meeting,
never thinking for a moment that her boss was squatting on this
motorway embankment with a bloody mouth.

His shoulders began to shake, a rapid tremor that set off his dia-
phragm. With an effort Maitland mastered the spasm. He swallowed back the phlegm that choked his throat and stared down at
the Jaguar, thinking again about the crash. It had been stupid of
him to ignore the speed limit. Eager to see Catherine again, he was
looking forward to relaxing in their cool, formal house with its large
white rooms. After three days with Helen Fairfax, in this sensible
woman doctor's warm and comfortable apartment, he had felt almost suffocated.

Standing up, Maitland edged sideways across the slope. Ten feet
above him was the hard shoulder of the motorway, and the palisade
of wooden trestles. Maitland tossed his briefcase up the slope. Moving like a crab on his feet and forearms, he climbed the more shallow soil, reached both hands on to the concrete shoulder and pulled
himself on to the road.

Exhausted by the climb, Maitland sat down unsteadily on a
wooden trestle. He brushed the dirt on his hands against his trousers. The briefcase and raincoat lay at his feet in a grimy bundle like

the luggage of a tramp. Sweat bathed his shirt inside the jacket, soaking through the fabric. The blood was thick in his mouth, but he sucked it back without a pause.

He stood up and turned to face the oncoming traffic. Three lines of vehicles sped towards him. They emerged from the tunnel below the overpass and accelerated along the fast bend. The rush hour had begun. Magnified by the roof and walls of the overpass, the noise reverberated off the concrete roadway around Maitland, drowning his first shouts. Now and then an interval of fifty feet appeared between the speeding vehicles, but even during these first minutes as Maitland stood there, waving his briefcase and raincoat, the hundreds of cars carrying their homeward drivers pressed closer together, almost bumper to bumper.

Maitland lowered the briefcase, watching the traffic roar past him. The red pinewood trestles had been knocked back by the speeding vehicles into a loose line. Lower in the western sky, the strong sun shone directly into the drivers' eyes as they emerged from the overpass into the fast right-hand bend.

Maitland looked down at himself. His jacket and trousers were stained with sweat, mud and engine grease—few drivers, even if they did notice him, would be eager to give him a lift. Besides, it would be almost impossible to slow down here and stop. The pressure of the following traffic, free at last from the long tailbacks that always blocked the Westway interchange during the rush hour, forced them on relentlessly.

Trying to position himself more conspicuously, Maitland edged along the narrow road shoulder. No pedestrian or emergency verge had been provided along this fast bend, and the cars speeding past him at sixty miles an hour were no more than three or four feet away. Still carrying the raincoat and briefcase, he moved along the

line of trestles, steering each one out of his way. He waved his hat
in the exhaust-filled air, shouting over his shoulder into the engine
noise.

'Emergency . . . ! Stop . . . ! Pull over . . . !'

Two trestles kicked together by a passing truck blocked his
way. The lines of traffic swept by, swerving under the route indicators towards the junction ahead. Brake lights pumped, and the
sunlight flared off the windshields in electric lances.

A horn blared warningly behind Maitland as he climbed around
the trestles. A car plunged within inches of his right hip, an angry
passenger whirling in a window. Maitland pulled himself back, and
saw the white hull of a police car in the far lane. It was moving at a
steady fifty miles an hour, a few feet behind the bumper of the car
in front, but the driver looked over his shoulder at Maitland.

'Slow down . . . ! Police . . . !'

Maitland waved both the hat and briefcase, but the police car
had been carried away by the rush of traffic. Trying to follow it on
foot, Maitland was almost hit by the fender of a passing taxi. A
black limousine swept towards him out of the tunnel, the uniformed
chauffeur seeing Maitland at the last moment.

Realizing that he would be crushed against the trestles, Maitland moved away from them. His right hand smarted from a passing blow. The skin had been torn by a piece of sharp windshield or
wing-mirror trim. He wrapped the blood-stained handkerchief
around it.

Three hundred yards away, beyond the eastern entrance of the
overpass, was the call box of an emergency telephone, but he knew
that he would be killed if he tried to walk through the tunnel. Maitland edged back along the hard shoulder and took up his position

at the point where the Jaguar had left the road. He put on his raincoat and buttoned it neatly, straightened his hat and waved calmly at the passing vehicles.

He was still standing there as dusk began to fall. Headlamps swerved past him, their beams cutting across his face. Horns blared endlessly as the three lines of vehicles, taillights flaring, moved towards the junction. The rush hour was in full swing. As Maitland stood weakly by the roadside, waving with a feeble hand, it seemed to him that every vehicle in London had passed and re-passed him a dozen times, the drivers and passengers deliberately ignoring him in a vast spontaneous conspiracy. He was well aware that no one would stop for him, at least until the rush hour was over at eight o'clock. Then, with luck, he might be able to attract the attention of a solitary driver.

Maitland lifted his watch into the glare of the passing head-lamps. It was seven forty-five. His son would long since have reached home alone. Catherine would either have gone out or be making dinner for herself, assuming that he had decided to stay on in London with Helen Fairfax.

Thinking of Helen, ophthalmoscope in the breast pocket of her white coat, peering critically into the eyes of some small child at her clinic, Maitland looked down at the wound on his hand. He was now more tired and shaken than at any time since the crash. Even in the warm, exhaust-filled air he shivered irritably; he felt as if his entire nervous system was being scraped by invisible knives, his nerves drawn through their slings. His shirt clung to his chest like a wet apron. At the same time a cold euphoria was coming over him.

He assumed that this light-headedness revealed the first symptoms of carbon monoxide poisoning. He waved at the cars lunging past him in the darkness, and tottered to and fro like a drunken man.

An articulated fuel tanker bore down on him along the outer lane, its yellow bulk almost filling the tunnel below the overpass. As it laboured around the bend the driver saw Maitland staggering between his headlamps. Air brakes hissed and slammed. Maitland side-stepped casually out of the tanker's way, took off his hat and tossed it under the massive rear wheels. Laughing to himself, Maitland watched it vanish.

'Hey . . . !' He gestured with his briefcase. 'My hat—you've got my hat . . . !'

Horns blared around him. A taxi pulled almost to a halt, the fender brushing Maitland's legs. Glaring down at Maitland, the driver tapped his forehead as he surged away. Maitland waved him on gallantly. He knew already that he was too exhausted to control himself. His one hope was that he might become so deranged that people would stop simply to prevent him from damaging their cars. He looked at the blood from his mouth on the back of his fingers, but flung the hand away and turned to the passing traffic. Gazing up at the maze of concrete causeways illuminated in the night air, he realized how much he loathed all these drivers and their vehicles.

'Stop . . . !'

He shook his blood-smeared fist at an elderly woman driver watching him suspiciously over her steering wheel.

'Yes, you . . . ! You can go! Take your damned car away! No—stop!'

He kicked a wooden trestle into the road, laughing as a passing truck knocked it back at him, jarring his left knee. He pushed out another.

His voice rose to a harsh shout above the traffic sounds, a bitter, primal scream.

'Catherine . . . ! Catherine . . . !'

With cold anger he shouted her name at the cars, screaming it like a child into the swerving headlamps. He lurched into the roadway again, blocking the outer lane and waving his briefcase like a demented racetrack official. Surprisingly, the traffic responded to him, thinning out slightly. For the first time a gap appeared in the stream of vehicles, and he could see through the tunnel to the Westway interchange.

Across the road from him was the central reservation, a narrow island four feet wide with a maintenance walk between the crash barriers. Maitland leaned against a trestle, trying to rally all his powers of self-control. He was aware of half his mind revelling in this drunken tantrum, but with an effort mastered himself. If he could cross the road, he would then be able to walk back to the Westway interchange and find an emergency telephone.

He straightened himself, annoyed that he had wasted time. Clearing his head, he waited for a break in the traffic stream. A dozen cars moved towards him in procession, followed by a second group, an airline coach taking up the rear. A breakdown truck towing a damaged van roared past Maitland, blocking his vision as he leaned back in the darkness, watching the play of headlamps in the approaches to the tunnel.

The road was clear except for a two-decker car transporter. The driver signalled to Maitland, as if prepared to offer him a lift. Maitland ignored him, waiting impatiently as the long stern section of the transporter lumbered by. The road was clear before the next set of approaching headlamps. Gripping the briefcase, he ran forward across the road.

He was halfway across the road when he heard the blare of a warning horn. Over his shoulder he saw the low hull of a white sportscar, almost invisible behind its unlit headlamps. Maitland stopped and turned back, but the skidding car was already on him, the young driver wrestling with the wheel as he lost control. Maitland felt the car rush through the air towards him. Before he could shout the car had plunged into a wooden trestle which Maitland had kicked into the road. The pinewood frame hurled against him. He felt his legs knocked away and was flung backwards through the dark air.

3

injury and exhaustion

'...Catherine...Catherine...'

The sound of his wife's name moved through the silent grass. Lying at the foot of the embankment, Maitland listened to the echoes of the syllables inside his head. As they roused him he realized that he had spoken the name himself. The faint sounds were audible in the darkness. The traffic noises had gone, and the embankment above him was quiet. Far away, beyond the central drum of the Westway interchange, an overnight truck driver steered his vehicle northwards, its engine labouring.

Maitland lay back in the darkness, his head resting against the soft slope of the embankment. His legs were hidden in the long grass. A hundred yards away, the three lanes of the feeder road were deserted. The route indicators towered above the unvarying yellow glow of the sodium lights. Involuntarily, as he thought about his wife's name, Maitland looked towards the west. Silhouetted against the evening corona of the city, the dark façades of the high-rise apartment blocks hung in the night air like rectangular planets.

For the first time since his accident, Maitland's head felt clear. The bruises on his temple and upper jaw, like the injuries to his legs and abdomen, were defined and localized, leaving his mind free. Already he knew that his right leg was severely damaged. A massive contusion was spreading from the hip down the outer surface of the thigh. Through the torn fabric of his trousers he touched the tender skin, raised by a leaking weal that wet his hand. The hip joint appeared to have been driven into the basin of his pelvis, and the displaced nerves and blood vessels throbbed through the torn musculature as they tried to reassemble themselves.

Maitland examined the damaged thigh with both hands. It was one forty-five a.m. Twenty yards away, the silver roof of the Jaguar reflected the distant lights of the motorway. He sat up, clenching his fists as he cut off his involuntary cry. He realized that the energy left to him was finite, perhaps half an hour of extended effort. He turned on to his side, drew his left leg out of the grass and lifted himself into a kneeling position.

Gasping at the night air, he no longer tried to control himself. He leaned helplessly against the embankment, hands deep in the cold soil. A faint dew already covered his torn suit, chilling his skin. He looked up at the steep slope, for a moment laughing aloud at himself.

'How the hell am I supposed to climb that . . . ? Might as well be Mount Everest.'

As he crouched there, trying to grapple with the pain from his injured hip, his whole situation seemed to Maitland like a bad joke that had got out of hand. A defective tyre wall, a bang on the head, and he had suddenly exited from reality. He thought of Helen Fairfax asleep in her flat, as always on the left side of the double bed that filled the minute bedroom, her head lying on the right-hand pillow, as if she had deputised the various sections of her body to represent both herself and Maitland. Curiously enough, this calm and capable woman doctor was a restless dreamer. By comparison, Catherine would be sleeping quietly in her white bedroom, a bar of moonlight across her pale throat. In fact, the whole city was now asleep, part of an immense unconscious Europe, while he himself crawled about on a forgotten traffic island like the nightmare of this slumbering continent.

Headlamps flared against the roof of the overpass tunnel. A car hummed along the silent roadway.

'Help . . . Stop . . .'

Maitland waved one hand without thinking. He listened to the car fade away, carrying its comfortable driver, latchkey securely in his pocket, to a warm suburban bed.

'Right . . . Let's try again . . .'

He climbed two feet up the slope, dragging the injured leg behind him, before collapsing into the soft earth. Even this small exertion had multiplied the pain in his hip socket. Unable to move, he knelt with his face in the broken soil, the cold earth against his cheek. Already he knew that he would never be able to climb the embankment, but he tried to drag himself up the slope, scooping armfuls of the soft earth from his path, forcing himself across the crumbling surface like a wounded snake.

'Catherine . . .'

For the last time he whispered her name, well aware that in some obscure way he was blaming her for his plight, for the pain in his injured leg, and for the cold night air that lay over his body like a damp shroud. A profound sense of depression had come over him, replacing the brief surge of confidence he had felt. Not only would Catherine assume that he was spending the night with Helen

Fairfax, but she would not particularly care. Yet, he himself had almost deliberately created this situation, as if preparing the ground for his crash ...

Night and silence settled over the motorway system. The sodium lights shone down on the high span of the overpass, rising into the air like some disused back entrance to the sky. Maitland lifted himself on to his left leg, supporting himself on his arms against the slope of the embankment. His right leg hung in front of him like a dead animal lashed to his belt. The long grass swayed in the night air, a corridor of crushed blades marking the route he had taken that afternoon. Hobbling along, the injured thigh held in both hands, he pressed on through the grass.

The silver fuselage of his car appeared among the shabby wrecks. Half-veiled by the grass, their rusting hulls were almost invisible. Maitland reached the rear door. Exhausted by the effort, he was about to lift himself into the back seat when he remembered the carton of wine bottles.

He pulled himself round to the rear of the car and unlocked the trunk. He lifted out one of the bottles of white Burgundy and fumbled with the wrapper. Opening the tool kit, he took out the adjustable spanner. On the second blow he struck the neck from the bottle. The clear liquid splashed around his feet in the cold air.

Sitting unsteadily in the rear seat of the Jaguar, Maitland drank his first mouthfuls of the warm Burgundy. He winced as the alcohol stung his cut mouth and gums. Within seconds the wine flushed his chest, and he could feel the pulse thudding in his injured thigh. Stretching his leg out on the seat, Maitland methodically drank his way down the bottle. Gradually he felt the pain in his hip begin to recede. He was soon too drunk to be able to focus on his wristwatch and gave up all sense of time. Stirred by the night air, the grass pressed closer against the windows, shutting out the embankments of the motorways. Maitland lay with the bottle in his hands, his head resting against the window pillar. One by one the points of pain that covered his chest and legs like a series of constellations began to fade, and the atlas of wounds into which his body had been transformed went out like a dead sky.

Mastering his self-pity, he thought again of Catherine and his son. He remembered his cold euphoria as he tottered about on the motorway, screaming his wife's name at the cars. If anything, he should have thanked her for marooning him here. Most of the happier moments of his life had been spent alone—student vacations touring Italy and Greece, a three-month drive around the United States after he qualified. For years now he had re-mythologized his own childhood. The image in his mind of a small boy playing endlessly by himself in a long suburban garden surrounded by a high fence seemed strangely comforting. It was not entirely vanity that the framed photograph of a seven-year-old boy in a drawer of his desk at the office was not of his son, but of himself. Perhaps even his marriage to Catherine, a failure by anyone else's standards, had succeeded precisely because it recreated for him this imaginary empty garden.

Nursing himself from the jagged bottle, he fell asleep three hours before dawn.

4

the water reservoir

He woke in broad daylight. The grass brushed against the quarter window by his head, blades dancing an urgent minuet as if they had been trying to wake him for some time. A panel of warm sunshine crossed his body. Unable to move for several seconds, he wiped the oil-smeared dial of his watch. It was eight twenty-five a.m. He lay sprawled stiffly across the back seat of the car. The motorway embankments were hidden from him, but a steady drumming, as threatening and yet in some way as reassuring as the soundtrack of a familiar nightmare, reminded him where he was.

The morning rush hour was under way, thousands of vehicles pouring back into central London. Horns sounded above the guttural roar of diesel engines and the unbroken boom of cars passing through the overpass tunnel.

The wine bottle lay under his right arm, its broken neck cutting into his elbow. Maitland sat up, remembering the anaesthesia which the wine had brought him. He could remember as well, like a degraded memory hiding itself in the back of his mind, the brief outburst of self-pity.

Maitland looked down at himself, barely recognizing the derelict figure sitting in the rear seat. His jacket and trousers were smeared with oil and blood. Engine grease covered the weal on his right hand where it had been struck by a passing car. His right thigh and hip had swollen into a massive contusion, and the head of his thighbone now seemed to be fused into the damaged pelvic socket. Maitland leaned over the front seat. Bruises and tender pressure-points covered his body like the percussion stops of an overstressed musical instrument.

'Maitland, no one's going to believe this . . .' The words, spoken aloud as a self-identification signal, merely made him aware of the damage to his mouth. Massaging the bruised gums, he smiled to himself with weary humour and peered at his face in the driving mirror. A livid bruise ran diagonally across the right side of his face like one half of an exaggerated handlebar moustache.

Time to get out of here . . . He looked round at the motorway embankment. The roofs of airline buses and high-topped trucks moved along the eastbound carriageway. The westbound lanes were almost empty. A delivery vehicle and two passenger coaches sped past on their way to the suburbs. Once he had climbed the embankment he would soon flag down a driver.

'Find a phone booth—Hammersmith Hospital—ring Catherine and the office . . .' Itemizing this checklist, Maitland opened the door and eased himself into the sunlight. He carried his right leg in both hands like a joint of meat and lifted it out on to the ground. He leaned unsteadily against the door, exhausted by this small effort. Deep spurs of pain reached from his hip into his groin and buttocks. Standing still, he could just balance himself on the injured leg. He clung to the roof gutter of the car and looked at the traffic moving along the motorway. The drivers had lowered their sun vizors, shielding their eyes from the morning sunlight. None of them would notice the haggard figure standing among the abandoned cars.

The cold air drummed at Maitland's chest. Even in the pale sunlight he felt cold and worn. Only his heavy physique had brought him through the crash and the injuries on the motorway. A stolen sportscar, unlit headlamps, an unlicensed driver—ten to one the young man at the wheel would not report hitting Maitland.

He lifted his injured leg and placed it in the grass in front of himself. He thought of the wine in the Jaguar's trunk, but he knew that the Burgundy would go straight to his head. Forget the wine, he told himself. Collapse into this long grass and no one will ever find you. You'll lie there and die.

Swinging his arms out, he managed to jump forward around the injured leg. He grasped at the long grass to steady himself.

'Maitland, this is going to take all day . . .'

He made a second step. Gasping for breath, he watched an airline coach move westwards along the motorway. None of the passengers looked down at the island. Gathering himself, Maitland made three more steps, almost reaching the blue hull of a saloon car lying on its side. As he stretched out a hand to the rusty chassis his injured leg tripped against a discarded tyre. His left knee buckled, dropping him into the long grass.

Maitland lay without moving in this damp bower. As he caught his breath he wiped the moisture from the grass on to his bruised mouth. He was still twenty feet from the embankment—even if he were to reach it he would never be able to climb the steep and un-packed slope.

He sat up, lifting himself on his hands through the grass. The rusty axle of the saloon car rose into the air above his head. The tyres and engine had been removed, and the exhaust pipe hung loosely from the expansion box. Maitland reached up and began to shake the pipe with his hands. He wrenched it from the bracket and pulled the six-foot section of rusty tubing from behind the rear axle. His strong arms bent one end into a crude handle.

'Right . . . ! Now we'll get somewhere . . .' Already Maitland felt his confidence returning. He hoisted himself on to this make-shift crutch and swung himself along, his injured leg clearing the ground.

He reached the foot of the embankment, and waved with one arm, shouting at the few cars moving along the westbound carriage-way. None of the drivers could see him, let alone hear his dry-throated croak, and Maitland stopped, conserving his strength. He tried to climb the embankment, but within a few steps collapsed in a heap on the muddy slope.

Deliberately, he turned his back to the motorway and for the first time began to inspect the island.

'Maitland, poor man, you're marooned here like Crusoe—If you don't look out you'll be beached here for ever . . .'

He had spoken no more than the truth. This patch of aban-doned ground left over at the junction of three motorway routes was literally a deserted island. Angry with himself, Maitland lifted the crutch to strike this meaningless soil.

He hobbled back towards his car. Twenty yards to the west of the breaker's yard he mounted a slight rise. Here he paused to

examine the perimeter of the island, searching for a service staircase or access tunnel. Below the overpass the wire-mesh fence ran
in an unbroken screen from one concrete embankment to the
other. The slope up to the feeder road was more than thirty feet
high and even steeper than the embankment of the motorway.
Where the two roads met, at the western apex, the earth slopes
gave way to vertical concrete walls.

Maitland swung himself back to his car, stopping every few
paces to beat down the long grass that thrust itself at him. When he
reached the car he unlocked the trunk and methodically counted
the five bottles of Burgundy, lifting each one from the carton in turn
as if this potent liquor represented the one point of reality left
to him.

He reached for the heavy spanner. Well, Maitland, he told himself, it's a little early for a drink, but the bar's open. Wait a minute,
though. Think, you need water.

As the morning sunlight steepened, warming his cold body, he
reminded himself again that even a few mouthfuls of the wine on
an unfed stomach would throw him into a drunken stupor. Somewhere among these cars there would be water.

The radiator. Slamming down the lid of the trunk, Maitland
picked up his crutch and swung himself to the front of the car. He
edged himself under the fender, with his bruised hands searched
among the brake lines and supension units for the lower edge of the
radiator. He found the stopcock and forced the tap, cupping the
liquid that jetted out.

Glycol! He spat away the bitter fluid and stared at the green stain
on his palm. The sharp tang of rusty water made his throat ache.

Already he sensed his reflexes quickening. He leaned across the
driving seat and released the hood catch. He pulled himself upright,

lifted the heavy hood and searched the engine compartment. His hands seized the water reservoir of the windshield washers. With one end of the crutch he twisted off the metal armature and ripped away the leads from the plastic canister.

It was almost full, holding nearly a pint of clear water. As he tasted the cool stream Maitland rested against the car, waving the crutch at the vehicles moving along the motorway. Small achievement though it was, the discovery of the water had recharged his confidence and determination. During his first hours on the island he had been too quick to assume that help would automatically arrive, that even a feeble gesture such as waving to a passing car would bring instant rescue.

He drank half the water, carefully bathing his injured mouth. He felt pleasantly light-headed, the water exciting his nerves and arteries like an electric stimulant. Hobbling around the car, he tapped the roof with almost child-like humour. He eased himself on to the trunk and sat there, looking across the uneven surface of the island at the wire-mesh fence. There were more than enough tools in the Jaguar's kit to wrench a hole through the mesh.

Laughing quietly to himself, Maitland lay against the rear window of the Jaguar. For some reason he felt a sudden and overwhelming sense of relief. He raised the canister into the air, and shook the clear liquid. He was certain now that he would escape. Despite his injuries and the damage to the car, his fears that he might be stranded for ever on the island seemed almost paranoid.

He was still laughing several minutes later when a passing driver in an open-topped car slowed down along the westbound carriageway. The driver, a uniformed American serviceman, looked down good-humouredly at Maitland, whom he clearly assumed to be a

tramp or drifter enjoying his first drink of the day. He gestured with
his thumb at Maitland, offering him a lift. Before Maitland could
control himself and realize that this was the only motorist since his
crash prepared to stop for him, the driver had waved courteously
and accelerated away.

5

the perimeter fence

Taking himself in hand like a weary drill sergeant, Maitland clambered down from the trunk of the Jaguar. He ignored the pain in his thigh and propped himself roughly against the car, waving the crutch and trying to call back the vanished driver. Sober now, he looked with disgust at his injured leg and ragged clothes, angry with himself for having given way to a moment of juvenile hysteria. As well as breaking up his car, the crash seemed to have jolted his brain loose from its moorings.

Maitland leaned his right armpit on to the metal crutch. He realized that he was unequipped to carry out any but the simplest physical activities. The grimy and crippled figure whose distorted reflection glimmered in the trunk lid exactly summed up his position on the island, marooned among these concrete causeways with almost no practical skills or resources.

Few psychological ones, for that matter, Maitland reflected. These days one needed a full-scale emergency kit built into one's brain, plus a crash course in disaster survival, real and imagined.

'Wrench, box spanner, wheel brace . . .' Maitland searched methodically through the tool kit. He spoke aloud to himself as if bullying along an incompetent recruit, exploiting his irritation with himself.

When he had loaded the tools into his jacket pockets he straightened the crutch and set off towards the overpass, ignoring the cars that moved along the motorway. It was shortly after nine o'clock, and the traffic had slackened after the morning rush hour. Already the warm sunlight was drawing from the damp grass the faint yellow haze that had hung over the island the previous afternoon, blurring the perimeter walls.

As he swung himself along, Maitland remembered that Catherine was collecting her new car that morning from the Japanese distributors. Helen Fairfax would be busy in the paediatric clinic at Guy's—ironically, neither would try to telephone him, each assuming that Maitland had spent the night with the other. For that matter, no one at his office would be particularly alarmed by his absence, taking for granted that he was ill or away on some urgent business. Maitland had trained his staff to accept his comings and goings without question. Several times he had flown to the United States, deliberately not notifying the office until his return. Even if he were away for a week his secretary would not feel concerned enough to call Catherine or Helen.

Painfully, his swing upset by the uneven ground, Maitland hobbled towards the wire-mesh fence. Below the grass he could identify the outlines of building foundations, the ground plans of Edwardian terraced houses. He passed the entrance to a World War II air-raid shelter, half-buried by the earth and gravel brought in to fill the motorway embankments.

By the time he reached the fence, deep within the shadow of the overpass, Maitland was exhausted. He leaned his crutch against the fence and sat down on the black earth. From his pockets he took out the wrench, box spanner and pliers. The heavy metal tools had dragged at his shoulders, bumping against his bruised chest and abdomen.

No grass grew under the overpass. The damp earth was dark with waste oil leaking from the piles of refuse and broken metal drums on the far side of the fence. The hundred-yard-long wire wall held back mounds of truck tyres and empty cans, broken office furniture, sacks of hardened cement. Builder's forms, bales of rusty wire and scrapped engine parts were heaped so high that Maitland doubted whether he would be able to penetrate this jungle of refuse even if he could cut through the fence.

Still sitting, he turned to face the wire. High above him, almost contiguous with the clear April sky, was the concrete span of the overpass, its broad deck reverberating faintly under the pressure of the passing traffic. Holding the pliers in both hands, he worked away at a metal link, testing the steel cord against the teeth. In the dim light he saw that he had made only a faint notch. Maitland shivered in the cold air. Moving the wrench and box spanner along the ground, he edged towards the steel post ten feet away. Here the adjacent sections of wire were pinned to the post by a continuous steel flange bolted on to a backing plate by self-locking nuts.

Adjusting the spanner, Maitland worked away at one of the nuts. He was now too weak even to get a secure grip on the head, let alone put any pressure to bear. He looked up at the high wall of the fence—ten years earlier, perhaps ten days earlier, he would have been strong enough to climb the fence with his bare hands.

He threw down the spanner, and scratched with the wrench at the damp ground. Although slick with oil, the dark earth was as impenetrable as sodden leather. To dig a trench below the fence he would need to excavate at least a cubic metre of stony soil, force his way through a ten-feet-high pile of truck tyres, each of which weighed a hundred pounds.

The dark air bit at his bruised lungs. Shivering in his damp clothes, Maitland replaced the tools in his pocket. As he emerged into the sunlight, the deep grass waved around his thighs, as if trying to transfer some of its warmth to him. Maitland stared unsteadily at the distant embankments of the motorway system. He had not eaten now for nearly twenty-four hours and the first severe hunger pangs, so far blunted by the shock of the accident, made his head reel. With an effort he focused his eyes on the roof of the Jaguar. The car was barely visible above the grass, which seemed to have grown several inches during his abortive journey to the wire-mesh fence.

Rallying himself, he set off across the island towards its southern perimeter. Every ten paces he stopped and beat a pathway through the heavy nettles with the crutch. He reached a low wall, and climbed a flight of steps that lifted into the air from the remains of a garden path. These ruins were all that remained of a stucco Victorian house pulled down years earlier.

The surface of the island was markedly uneven. Covering everything in its mantle, the grass rose and fell like the waves of a brisk sea. A broad valley ran down the central spine of the island, marking out the line of a former neighbourhood high street. On either side, the grass climbed over blunted ledges and parapets, overran the empty areaways.

Maitland crossed the central valley and mounted the slope on the southern side, picking a defile between two small elders that struggled with the invading nettles. The crutch rang out against a metal object underfoot, an iron plaque set into a fallen gravestone. He was standing in an abandoned churchyard. A pile of worn headstones lay to one side. A series of shallow gullies marked the row of graves, and Maitland assumed that the bones had been removed to an ossuary.

The high embankment of the feeder road rose above him. The traffic moving past thirty feet above his head was concealed by the crash barrier. The drone of engines blended into the distant sounds of the morning city.

Maitland swung himself along the foot of the embankment. The ground was littered with cigarette packs, stubs of burnt-out cigars, confectionery wrappers, spent condoms and empty matchbooks. Fifty yards in front of him the concrete caisson of a traffic sign protruded from the embankment.

Maitland quickened his step, jerking himself across the soft soil. As he guessed, a gutter ran along the foot of the caisson. The narrow gully, washed clear of all refuse by the rain, led around the concrete wall to the mouth of a drainage culvert. Behind its cast-iron grille the storm-tunnel ran into the embankment, emerging a hundred feet away.

Maitland tapped the grille with the crutch. He accepted without comment that he would not be able to unbolt the heavy metal structure. He stared down at the bars, for some reason wondering if they were wide enough apart for him to slip his hands between them. He turned and hobbled away through the refuse, stirring the cigarette packs with the crutch.

As he plodded along, head down, he broke into a flat and unemotional rage, ranting to himself at the unseen vehicles overhead.

'Stop . . . ! For God's sake, I've had enough . . . !'

When there was no reply he calmly continued on his way. The

light air swirled the candy wrappers around his injured leg. As he crossed the island the grass weaved and turned behind him, moving in endless waves. Its corridors opened and closed as if admitting a large and watchful creature to its green preserve.

6

the rainstorm

During the warm noon, Maitland slept inside his car. On the rear seat beside him were the water canister and a fresh bottle of Burgundy. He woke at two o'clock, as the driver of a dumper truck crossing the overpass switched his air-brakes on and off in a series of sharp detonations. Although the exertion of crossing the island had re-inflamed his injured leg, Maitland's head felt clear. The sharp hunger pangs reached up from his abdomen into his throat like a steel hand, but he sat quietly in the rear seat. Resting through the early afternoon, he took stock of himself.

He realized, above all, that the assumption he had made repeatedly since his arrival on the island—that sooner or later his crashed car would be noticed by a passing driver or policeman, and that rescue would come as inevitably as if he had crashed into the central reservation of a suburban dual carriageway—was completely false, part of that whole system of comfortable expectations he had carried with him. Given the peculiar topography of the island, its mantle of deep grass and coarse shrubbery, and the collection of

ruined vehicles, there was no certainty that he would ever be noticed at all. Given, too, the circumstances of his private and professional life, that once-so-convenient division between his wife and
Dr Helen Fairfax, it might be at least a week before anyone was
sufficiently suspicious to call the police. Yet even the most astute
detective retracing Maitland's route from his office would be hard
put to spot his car shielded by this sea of grass.

Maitland loosed his trousers and inspected his injured thigh.
The joint had stiffened, and the heavy bruising and broken blood
vessels gleamed through the overlay of oil and dirt.

Nursing his injured mouth, he drank the last of the tacky water
in the windshield reservoir. He scanned the office blocks visible
through the haze over central London. A conference he had been
due to attend would now be re-assembling after lunch—did any of
the delegates have any idea what had happened to him? Even if he
were rescued now, it would be several days at least, and possibly
weeks, before he returned to work. He thought of the chain of ap-
pointments missed, cancelled client meetings, a committee on
which he sat. Like a tocsin warning him reprovingly of all this,
Maitland's leg began to throb.

'Right—let's see what we've got . . .' Maitland roused himself,
mastering the mounting urge to sleep all the time. He swung himself round to the rear of the car. He could hear the traffic moving
along the motorway, but he ignored the vehicles, knowing that he
would only tire himself by trying to wave them down.

He lifted the lid of the trunk and opened his overnight case. The
vivid scent of his aftershave filled the air. He took out his patent
dress shoes and dinner jacket. The overnight case was almost literally a time capsule—he could easily reconstitute a past world from
these scents and surface textures.

He unclipped the blade from his razor, and cut his blue towel into strips. He soaked one of the strips in his aftershave. The tart cologne stung his injured hand, biting at the dozens of minute cuts and abrasions. Maitland cleaned away the dirt and oil that clotted the kidney-shaped wound running from the knuckle of his wrist to the ball of his thumb. He bandaged the hand with the towelling strips, locked the trunk and hobbled through the grass around the abandoned cars.

Five vehicles, wrecks left behind in the breaker's yard, lay in a semicircle around the Jaguar. The grass grew through the gaps in the rusting body panels, sprouting through the empty engine compartment of the overturned taxi. Dented fenders, a pile of bald tyres, a single bonnet hood, lay among the nettles. Maitland moved among them, now and then looking up at the embankment as he estimated what he would need to build a ramp.

Rain fell across Maitland's neck. He swung himself back to the Jaguar. The sun was hidden by the darkening cloud. Already it was raining heavily over central London. As he stepped into the car the cloudburst broke across the island. The gusts of rain-filled air levelled the swirling grass. The cars moving along the motorway were lashed by the rain, their headlamps flaring in the liquid darkness.

Maitland sat back in the rear seat, watching the rain hit the window glass three inches from his face. He stared passively at the storm, grateful that he had even the minimal shelter of this crashed car. The rain striking the bonnet danced back through the open windshield, the motes of spray hitting his face.

'Come on!' Deliberately striking his injured leg, Maitland opened the rear door. The dark rain lashed at his head, soaking his torn clothes as he pulled out his leg and struggled with the crutch, twice dropping it to the ground. As he swung himself across the

breaker's yard the whirling raindrops cut like shot through the thin
fabric of his jacket and trousers. Maitland turned his head, catching the rain in his open mouth as he lurched along.

He stumbled over the bald tyres and fell to his knees. Seizing
the loose bonnet hood he had noticed earlier, he struggled back to
his feet. Ignoring the rain stinging his cold skin, and the sodden
bandage on his right hand, he dragged the hood towards the Jaguar, lifted it on to the bonnet and jammed it upside down through
the open windshield.

He stood back as the first water rilled down the greasy metal
on to the instrument panel of the Jaguar. Leaning on the crutch,
Maitland shouted soundlessly to himself, an exultant madman in
the driving rain. His wet clothes clung to him like a dead animal.
He climbed into the car and crouched over the front seat with the
reservoir canister, steering the wavering stream of water that moved
down the upturned hood. The rain slackened when there was little
more than half a pint of bubble-filled water in the canister, but after
five minutes began again in a steady torrent.

By the time the storm ended, thirty minutes later, Maitland had
collected a full canister of water. All this while, as he crouched forward in his soaked clothes, bruised hands fumbling across the
front seat, Maitland talked aloud to himself, half aware that he was
bringing both Catherine and Helen Fairfax into these monologues,
sometimes mimicking their voices, allowing them to taunt him with
his incompetence. To keep himself awake, he deliberately strained
his injured leg, in some way identifying the pain with the image
in his mind of these two women.

'Good . . . nearly full, don't cut your mouth on this damned plastic. Not bad—two pints of water, enough for a couple of days.

Catherine wouldn't be impressed, though . . . She'd see the whole thing as some kind of over-extended joke. "Darling, you always have driven rather too fast, you know . . ." I'd like to see her here, as a matter of fact, how long would she last . . . ? Interesting experiment. Wait a minute, Maitland, they'd stop for *her*. Thirty seconds on that motorway and they'd be locked bumper to bumper all the way back to Westway. What the hell am I talking about? Why blame them, Maitland? The rain's going off . . . must get away from this island before my strength goes. Head hurts, might be concussion . . . cold here, bloody leg . . .'

As the sun came out again, its rays sweeping through the un-kempt grass like the tines of an invisible comb, Maitland shivered in his soaked clothes. He drank frugally from the reservoir bottle. The rainwater was well aerated but tasteless, and Maitland won-dered whether he had suffered some minor brain damage that had dulled his perception of taste. He knew that his physical strength was moving along a perceptible downhill gradient. Losing interest in the water which he had worked so hard to collect, he climbed from the car and opened the trunk.

Maitland stripped off his jacket and shirt. The wet rags fell from his hands into the pool of muddy water at his feet. It was now little more than twenty-four hours since his accident, but the skin of his arms and chest had blossomed into a garden of bruises, vividly co-loured weals and markings. Maitland put on the spare dress shirt, and buttoned on the dinner jacket, turning up the collar. He threw his wallet into the trunk and locked down the lid.

Even in the sunlight he felt frozen. In an effort to warm him-self, he forced the cork into the wine bottle and sipped at the Bur-gundy. For the next hour he hobbled between the breaker's yard and the embankment, carrying all the tyres and fenders he could find. The area around the cars soon became a quagmire in which he slid about like a scarecrow in his mud-spattered dinner jacket.

Around him the last of the day's sunlight fell on the deep grass, drawing the stems even further into the air. This luxuriant growth seemed to Maitland an almost conscious attempt to inundate him. He set the tyres into the slope of the embankment, laboriously cutting the earth away with the crutch. The rain-washed soil liquefied around him in a soft avalanche. The fenders sank through the surface. As the first sounds of the evening rush hour began, Maitland managed to climb halfway up the embankment, dragging the injured leg after him like a dying companion on a mountain wall.

The traffic drummed over his head, no more than twenty feet away, an unceasing medley of horns and engines. At intervals the high face of an airline bus sped past, the passengers visible behind their windows. Maitland waved to them as he sat in the shifting mud.

He was ten feet from the top, too exhausted to move forwards any further, when he saw that the palisade of wooden trestles had been replaced and strengthened. A few steps above his head, on the inverted beach that led up from the island, was the footprint of a steel-capped industrial boot, its stud marks visible in the fading light. Maitland counted five other imprints. Had the highway maintenance staff repositioned the damaged trestles? The workmen had come down the slope, presumably looking for any injured driver or pedestrian at the time when he was hobbling about on the far side of the island.

The sun fell behind the apartment blocks at White City. Giving up for the time being, Maitland crawled back to the car. As he clambered into the rear seat he knew that he was showing the first signs of fever. Hunched in the mud-stained dinner jacket, he clutched at the wine bottle, trying to warm himself. The traffic moved through the dusk, headlamps flaring under the route indicators. The siren of a police car howled its way through the dusk. Maitland waited for it to stop, and for the police crew to come down the embankment with a stretcher. In his aching head the concrete overpass and the system of motorways in which he was marooned had begun to assume an ever more threatening size. The illuminated route indicators rotated above his head, marked with meaningless destinations, the names of Catherine, his mother and his son.

By nine o'clock the bout of fever had passed. As the noise of the rush hour receded, Maitland revived himself with several mouthfuls of wine. Sitting forward over the front seat, he stared at the rain-splashed instrument panel, concentrating whatever intelligence and energy were left to him. Somehow he could still devise a means of escaping from the island. Half a mile to the west, the lights were shining in the apartment blocks, where hundreds of families were finishing their evening meals. Any one of them would clearly see a fire or flare.

Maitland watched the glowing arc of a cigarette butt thrown down the embankment from a passing car. At this point he realized that he was literally sitting on enough signal material to light up the entire island.

7

the burning car

Controlling his excitement, Maitland looked down at the curved roof of the fuel tank. He pushed aside the overnight case and the tool kit, and began to strike at the centre of the tank with the open jaws of the adjustable spanner. As the chips of paint stung his hands the exposed metal glinted in the darkness. The heavy-gauge steel inside its collision-resistant frame was too strong for him to perforate. Maitland dropped the spanner on to the muddy ground at his feet. A car approached through the tunnel of the overpass, its headlamps turning through the air twenty feet above his head. Maitland lowered himself to the ground and swivelled his head and shoulders under the rear fender. He searched for the stopcock under the tank.

How do you set fire to a car, he asked himslf. The cliché of a thousand films and TV plays. As he sat against the trunk in the dim light he tried to remember a single detailed episode. If he opened the stopcock the fuel would gush out on to the rain-sodden ground, evaporate and dilute itself within minutes. Besides, he had no matches. Some kind of spark was essential. Maitland looked over his shoulder at the dark hull of the car. He thought systematically about its electrical system—the high-voltage coil, the new battery, the distributor with its contact breaker . . . The car was alive with electrical points, even though the headlamp and brake-light circuit was out.

The cigarette lighter! Clambering to his feet, Maitland pulled himself round to the driving seat. Switching on the ignition, he tested the dashboard lights, watching them glow in the darkness. He pressed in the cigarette lighter. Ten seconds later it jumped back against his palm. The red glow warmed his broken hands like a piece of the sun. He lay back as it faded, falling asleep for a few seconds.

'Catherine . . . Catherine . . .' Murmuring her name aloud, he deliberately provoked himself to keep awake, playing on any feelings of guilt, hostility or affection he could rouse. Carrying the wrench, he clambered from the car. He slung aside the watercourse, lifted the Jaguar's bonnet and peered into the engine compartment.

'Fuel pump . . . right.' Maitland hammered with the wrench at the glass cone on the pump. On the fifth blow, when he was ready to give up, the glass fractured. Maitland smashed away the pieces as the gasolene spilled over the engine and dripped on to the ground. Intoxicated by the smell of the raw fuel, Maitland leaned over the engine, head swaying with relief and exhaustion. He tried to calm himself. Within minutes he would be saved, probably be on his way to hospital . . .

Maitland climbed back into the driving seat and switched on the ignition. The lights of the instrument panel, a faint glow in the cabin, were reflected in the lapels of his mud-smeared dinner jacket. From the dashboard locker he took out his London route map, and folded it into a two-foot-long spill. Satisfied, he turned the ignition

key and activated the starter motor. As the servo whined, turning
over the engine, the car rocked from side to side. Fed by the reservoir of fuel in the float chambers of the carburettors, the engine almost coughed into life. As he released the starter Maitland could
already smell the fuel being drawn from the tank by the pump and
flooding through the broken glass cap. He listened to it splashing
on to the ground below the car. He ran the starter motor for thirty
seconds, until the cabin of the car was filled with the fumes.

'Careful now . . . a lot of electrics around . . . roast to a crisp inside here . . .'

He turned on the ignition and pressed in the cigarette lighter,
steering his legs on to the ground through the door. When the
lighter jumped out he plucked it from the dashboard, pivoted in his
seat and lit the spill. He threw away the lighter and propelled himself on to the ground, the crutch in his left hand, the burning spill
held in the air above his head.

When he was six feet from the car he lay down in the damp
grass. Fuel dripped from the wet engine, forming a pool between
the wheels. Shielding his face with one arm, Maitland tossed the
burning map under the car.

A violent ball of flame erupted in the darkness, briefly illuminating the semicircle of cars in the breaker's yard. The engine
blazed hotly, burning fuel dripping from its glowing sides. Pools of
scattered fuel burned themselves out around the car. In the flame-
light he could see the high wall of grass around the yard, the blades
inclined forwards like the members of an eager audience.

The dark, heavy smoke of burning gasolene lifted around the
Jaguar's engine through the open bonnet. Already the first cars were
slowing down as they emerged from the overpass tunnel. Two
drivers cruised together along the motorway, watching the vivid

flames. Maitland lifted himself on to the crutch and swung himself towards them. He fell over twice, but each time pulled himself
back on to his feet.

'Stop . . . ! Slow down . . . ! Wait a minute . . . !'

An aircraft swept overhead, its navigation lights pulsing in the
rain-clouded sky. The pilot was throttling back on his final approach
to London Airport, and the noise of the four huge turbofans
drowned out the thin sounds of Maitland's voice. Leaping along like
an animated scarecrow, he watched the cars move away. Already
the flames were subsiding as the last of the fuel burned itself away.
Far from being the sustained conflagration he had hoped for, the
fire burning in the engine compartment already resembled a large
stove, an open brazier of the type used by scrap-metal workers.
From the foot of the embankment all that was visible was a bright
glow that illuminated the hulls of the overturned wrecks.

Hoarse and exhausted, Maitland reached the embankment in
a hobbling run, carried a few steps up the slope by his momentum.
He tottered back on to the level ground as a large American saloon
slowed down, almost stopping directly above him. The driver, a
young man with blond shoulder-length hair, was eating a sandwich.
He gazed down at Maitland as the last flames lifted from the Jaguar.
When Maitland gestured pleadingly, unable to shout any more, the
young man waved back, tossed away the sandwich and pressed
hard on the accelerator, carrying the long car into the darkness.

Maitland sat wearily on the embankment. Clearly this young
driver had assumed that the burning car was part of some tramp's
celebration, or a small fire lit to provide an evening meal. Even from
where he himself was sitting it was by no means clear that a car was
burning at all.

It was now ten o'clock, and the first lights were going out in the high-rise apartments. Too tired to move, and trying to decide where he could spend the night, Maitland lowered his eyes. Ten feet away from him was the white triangle of the discarded sandwich. Maitland stared at it, the pain in his injured leg forgotten.

Without thinking, he crawled towards the sandwich. He had not eaten for thirty-six hours, and found it difficult to focus his mind. He looked down at the two slices of bread, held together around their filling of chicken and salad cream by the semicircular impress of the young man's teeth.

Seizing the sandwich, Maitland devoured it. Intoxicated by the taste of animal fat and the moist texture of buttered bread, he made no effort to remove the grains of dirt. When he had finished the sandwich he licked the last drops of salad cream from his blackened fingers and searched the slope for any pieces of chicken that might have fallen out.

Picking up the crutch, he took himself back to the Jaguar. The flames had died down, and the last smoke from the engine rose through the dark air. A light rain was coming down, the drops hissing on the cylinder head.

The front of the car had been gutted. Maitland climbed into the back seat. Drinking steadily from the bottle of Burgundy, he gazed at the burnt-out instrument panel and steering wheel, and the front seats charred through to their springs.

Despite his failure in setting fire to his car, Maitland felt a quiet satisfaction that he had found the discarded sandwich. Small step though this was, it stood in his mind as yet another success he had won since being marooned. Sooner or later he would meet the island on equal terms.

He slept steadily until dawn.

8

the messages

The morning sunlight crossed the instrument panel of the car, creeping through the coils of blackened wiring. Around the smoke-streaked windows the tall grass swayed in the warm air. In these first minutes after he had woken, Maitland lay against the rear seat, looking through the smeared glass at the motorway embankment. He brushed at the mud caked across the lapels of his dinner jacket. It was eight ten a.m. He was surprised by the complete silence of the surrounding landscape, the uncanny absence of that relentless roar of rush-hour vehicles which had woken him the previous morning. It was almost as if some idle-minded technician responsible for maintaining the whole illusion of his marooning on the island had forgotten to switch on the sound.

Maitland stirred his cramped body. His swollen leg lay alongside him like the limb of some partly invisible companion. By contrast, the rest of his once-heavy physique had shrunk during the night. The bones of his shoulders and rib cage pointed through his bruised skin, as if trying to detach themselves from the surrounding musculature. Maitland ran his torn nails through the light beard beginning to cover his face. Already he was thinking of the chicken sandwich he had eaten before falling asleep. The bland, fatty taste of meat and salad cream still clung to his teeth.

Maitland sat forward over the front seat, peering down at the springs that protruded through the charred leather. Although he was now far weaker physically, his mind felt clear and alert. He knew that whatever he decided to do in his attempt to escape from the island, he must not exhaust himself. He remembered the hostility he had felt for his injured body, and the calculated way in which he had abused himself in order to keep going. From now on, he must relax a little, husband his self-confidence. It might take several hours to devise a means of escape, perhaps another day.

His basic needs, a few of which he could meet, were for water, food, shelter, and some kind of signalling device. He would never be able to escape from the island unaided—the embankments were too steep, and even if he could winch himself to the top he would be barely conscious by the time he climbed the balustrade. Tottering across the road, he might easily be killed by a passing truck.

Maitland pushed back the door and picked up the crutch. Even this small effort made his head swim. He leaned against the seat as the blades of crushed grass sprang through the open door, reaching into the car against his leg. The resilience of this coarse grass was a model of behaviour and survival.

Maitland vomited emptily against the door, watching the globes of silver mucus drip on to the carpet. He lifted himself unsteadily on to the crutch and leaned against the car, doubting whether he would be able to stand for long. The mud-smeared dinner jacket flapped around him in the light wind, several sizes too large for his gaunt shoulders.

He hobbled forward, inspecting the damage to the Jaguar. Patches of the grass around the car had been burned away, exposing circles of charred earth. The fire had destroyed the battery and engine wiring, burning through the instrument panel bulkhead into the front passenger compartment.

'Damned quiet . . .' Maitland murmured aloud to himself. No cars or airline buses moved along the motorways. The aerial balconies of the apartment blocks were deserted in the sunlight.

Where the devil was everyone? God . . . some kind of psychosis. Nervously, Maitland pivoted on the crutch. He hobbled across the charred earth, trying to find a single tenant of this abandoned landscape. Had a world war broken out overnight? Perhaps the source of a virulent plague had been identified somewhere in central London. During the night, as he lay asleep in the burnt-out car, an immense silent exodus had left him alone in the deserted city.

Three hundred yards to the west of the island's apex, beyond the junction of the motorway and the feeder road, a single figure appeared. An elderly man approached the island, pushing a light motorcycle along the eastbound carriageway. He was partly hidden by the central reservation, but in the bright sunlight Maitland could clearly see his long white hair swept back off his forehead on to his shoulders.

As he watched this old man pushing along his silent machine, Maitland was overcome by a sudden sense of fear that drove away all awareness of his hunger and exhaustion. By some nightmare logic he was convinced that the old man was coming for him, perhaps not now but by some circuitous route through the labyrinth of motorways, and that he would eventually arrive to summon Maitland to the point where he had crashed. Moreover, Maitland was certain that this machine he was wheeling was not in fact a light

motorcycle, but an horrific device of torture that the old man
brought with him on his endless journey around the world, and
against whose chain-driven wheels Maitland's already broken body
would be applied in a grim judgement by ordeal.

Galvanizing himself, Maitland began to hobble at random around
the breaker's yard, swaying and tottering in this circle of dead fire.
The man's white head was still visible along the eastbound carriageway, eyes fixed on the empty road curving ahead of him. His
shabby clothes and antique machine were illuminated by the sunlight.

   Maitland crouched in the grass, grateful to this deep bower for
hiding him from the approaching figure. He looked at his watch,
noticing the date dial at the same moment as an empty car transporter lumbered through the tunnel of the overpass, its diesel
braying.

   April 24th . . .

   Saturday! The weekend had begun. He had crashed on
Thursday afternoon, and had now spent two nights on the island.
It was Saturday morning, and this explained the silence and ab-
sence of traffic.

   Light-headed with relief, Maitland hobbled back to the Jaguar.
He drank some water to steady himself. The old man and his
motorcycle had gone, hidden somewhere beyond the overpass.
Maitland massaged his arms and chest, trying to master his trem-
bling. Had he imagined this solitary figure, conjuring up the spectre
of some infantile guilt?

   He looked around the perimeter of the island, carefully scan-
ning the embankments in case any falls of food had taken place dur-

ing the night. Parcels of newspaper, the bright tags of confectionery wrappers—somehow he must find something to eat. The four bottles of Burgundy would keep him going in an emergency, and there must be edible berries growing on the island, perhaps a forgotten allotment garden with a row of wild potatoes.

The caisson of the feeder road indicator sign caught his eye. The rain-washed concrete shone brightly in the sunlight like an empty noticeboard. A message scrawled across it in three-feet-high letters would be legible to drivers on the motorway . . .

Maitland swung himself around the car. He needed writing materials of some kind, or failing that, a tool sharp enough to scratch the concrete so that he could rub dirt into the scored surface.

The stench of burnt rubber and oil hung over the engine compartment. Maitland looked down at the blackened wiring hanging from the distributor. One by one, he pulled the terminals from the sparking plugs and filled his pockets with the burnt rubber guards.

Half an hour later he had crossed the island and was sitting beside the white slope of the caisson. His legs stretched in front of him like ragged poles. The effort of pushing through the long grass had soon exhausted Maitland. At places in the central valley the vegetation rose shoulder-high. Several times he had fallen over the stone walls and brickwork courses hidden beneath the grass, but he picked himself up and doggedly pushed ahead. By now he ignored the nettles that stung his legs through the torn fabric of his trousers, accepting these burning weals in the same way that he accepted his own weariness. By doing so he found he could concentrate on whatever task lay in front of him—the next painful push through a nettle bank, a difficult step across a tilting flag-stone. In some way, this act of concentration proved that he could dominate the island.

From the pockets of his dinner jacket he took out the plug caps and burnt rubber leads he had twisted from the engine. Like a child at play, Maitland set out the pieces of charred rubber in two rows in front of him.

He was too tired to stand, but he could reach to within four feet of the ground. Carefully, in wavering letters eighteen inches high, he marked up his message.

HELP INJURED DRIVER CALL POLICE

Leaning against the cold concrete, Maitland surveyed his handi-work. Like a dying pavement artist in a rich man's cast-off, he pulled the damp dinner jacket around his thin shoulders. But his hungry eyes soon turned their interest to the cigarette packs, tattered newspapers and refuse lying around him at the foot of the embankment.

Ten feet away from Maitland was a bundle of greasy newspa-per, tossed down during the night from a car or truck moving along the feeder road. Cooking oil leaked through the crushed pages. Pulling himself together, Maitland crawled towards the newspaper. He drew the bundle to him with the handle of the crutch. Fumbling in his hunger, he tore open the paper, over-whelmed by the smell of fried fish that clung to the smeary half-tone illustrations. The food had probably been bought by the driver at one of the all-night cafés that formed a small encamp-ment by the southern entrance to the Westway interchange.

All the fish had gone—however, as Maitland had guessed from

the neat way the parcel had been wrapped, it still held some twenty fried potatoes.

As he devoured these greasy fingers in his blackened hands, the first rain of the day struck the dust around his legs. Chuckling to himself, Maitland stuffed the paper into the pocket of his dinner jacket. He lifted himself to his feet and moved away through the deep grass. The roads around the island were deserted again. Carried by a brisk north-east wind, armadas of dark cloud swept overhead. Alone in this concrete landscape, Maitland tottered along, hoping to reach the shelter of his car. He looked back briefly at the letters he had chalked on the embankment, but they were barely visible above the grass.

The rain gusted across him before he could reach the central valley, forcing him to stop and cling to the crutch. Maitland looked down at his waving hands, moving about in a meaningless semaphore as the rain streamed across them. He knew that he was not merely exhausted, but behaving in a vaguely eccentric way, as if he had forgotten who he was. Parts of his mind seemed to be detaching themselves from the centre of his consciousness.

He stopped to search for shelter. The grass seethed and whirled around him, as if sections of this wilderness were speaking to each other. Maitland let the rain lash his face, turning his head so that he could catch the drops in his mouth. Surrounded by the squalls of rain, he was tempted to stand there for ever, and only reluctantly pushed himself forward.

Losing his way, Maitland stumbled into a room-sized enclosure bounded by the nettles growing from the wall-courses of a ruined house. Standing in this stony garden, like the dead centre of a maze, he tried to find his bearings. The heavy rain clouds hung in dense curtains between himself and the motorway. The mud caked across his dinner jacket dissolved and ran into streams down his ragged trousers, exposing the blood-stained flank of his right thigh. Confused for a moment, Maitland squeezed his wrists and elbows, trying to identify himself.

'Maitland . . . !' he shouted aloud. 'Robert Maitland . . . !'

He clung to the metal crutch and hobbled from the garden. Twenty feet to his left, beyond a pile of galvanized iron sheets, was the ruined entrance to a basement doorway. Maitland vomited into the streaming rain. He wiped the phlegm from his mouth and swung himself over the stony ground. Worn steps ran down to the doorway, where a narrow entrance led under a tilting lintel into the open air.

Maitland dragged the sheets of galvanized iron towards the steps. Laying them carefully between the lintel and the top step, he built a crude roof, adjusting the sheets so that the slope carried away the streaming rain. He threw the crutch down the steps and eased himself under the roof of his new shelter.

Sitting on the steps as the rain drummed at the metal roof over his head, Maitland took off the dinner jacket and squeezed the sodden fabric in his bruised hands. The muddy water ran away between his fingers, as if he were washing out a child's football gear. He spread the jacket across the steps and massaged his shoulders, trying to draw a little warmth from the pressure of his hands. He could feel his fever returning, fed from the inflamed hip wound. Nonetheless, his success in building even this shabby shelter had revived him, rekindling his still unbroken determination to survive. As he was already well aware, it was this will to survive, to dominate the island and harness its limited resources, that now seemed a more important goal than escaping.

Maitland listened to the rain striking the galvanized iron. He remembered the house his parents had taken in the Camargue for their last summer together. The intense delta rain had fallen on the garage roof below the windows of the bedroom where he had happily spent most of the holiday. It was no coincidence that when he had first taken Helen Fairfax to the south of France they had gone straight to La Grande Motte, the futuristic resort complex on the coast a few miles away. Helen had quietly hated the hard, affectless architecture with its stylized concrete surfaces, nervous of Maitland's buoyant humour. At the time he had found himself wishing that Catherine were with him—she would have liked the ziggurat hotels and apartment houses, and the vast, empty parking lots laid down by the planners years before any tourist would arrive to park their cars, like a city abandoned in advance of itself.

Through the open doorway Maitland watched the pools of water covering the weed-grown basement into which the first floor had collapsed. A small printing shop had once been here, and a few copper-backed letterpress blocks lay around his feet. Maitland picked one up and examined the cloudy figures of a dark-suited man and a white-haired woman. As he listened to the rain he thought of his parents' divorce; the uncertainties of this period, when he was eight years old, seemed to be replicated in the negative image on the letterpress plate, in the reversed tones of this unknown man and woman.

An hour later, when the rain had ended, he climbed from his shelter. Holding tightly to the crutch, he hobbled back to the southern embankment. His fever continued to rise, and he gazed lightheartedly at the deserted causeways of the motorway.

When he reached the embankment and searched for the message he had scrawled on the white flank of the caisson, he found that all the letters had been obliterated.

9

fever

The last of the rain fell across Maitland's face. He stared at the remains of the message he had inscribed on the damp concrete. The letters had been reduced to black smudges, the smeared rubber running to the ground at his feet.

Trying to concentrate, Maitland searched the ground for his rubber markers. Had someone wiped the letters away? Uncertain of himself and his ability to reason clearly, Maitland leaned unsteadily against the metal crutch. The fever poured from his chest and lungs. He realized that the rounded smears were exactly like those of a windshield wiper. He looked round wildly at the island and its deserted motorway embankments. Was he still trapped inside his car? Was the entire island an extension of the Jaguar, its windshield and windows transformed by his delirium into these embankments? Perhaps the windshield wipers had jammed and were flicking to and fro as he lay forward on his crushed chest across the steering wheel, tracing some incoherent message on the steaming glass . . .

The sunlight broke through the white cumulus to the east of the island, illuminating the high embankment like a spotlight switched on to a stage set. A truck laboured along the feeder road, the rectangular pantechnicon of a furniture van visible above the balustrade.

Maitland turned his back on the vehicle. Suddenly he no longer cared about the message and the obliterated letters. He swung himself roughly through the waist-high grass, soaking the torn fabric of his trousers and dinner jacket against the rain-wet stems. In the over-bright sunlight the island and the concrete motorways glimmered with a hard vibrancy that surged through his crippled body. The grass flashed with an electric light, encircling his thighs and calves. The wet leaves wound across his skin, as if reluctant to release him. Maitland swung his injured leg over a ruined brick course. Somehow he must rally himself while he was still strong enough to move about.

No point in going back to the car, he told himself.

The grass seethed around him in the light wind, speaking its agreement.

'Explore the island now—drink the wine later.'

The grass rustled excitedly, parting in circular waves, beckoning him into its spirals.

Fascinated, Maitland followed the swirling motions, reading in these patterns the reassuring voice of this immense green creature eager to protect and guide him. The spiral curves swerved through the inflamed air, the visual signature of epilepsy. His own brain—the fever, perhaps damage to his cerebral cortex . . .

'Find a ladder . . . ?'

The grass lashed at his feet, as if angry that Maitland still wished to leave its green embrace. Laughing at the grass, Maitland patted it reassuringly with his free hand as he hobbled along, stroking the seething stems that caressed his waist.

Almost carried by the grass, Maitland climbed on to the roof of an abandoned air-raid shelter. Resting here, he inspected the island more carefully. Comparing it with the motorway system, he saw that it was far older than the surrounding terrain, as if this triangular patch of waste ground had survived by the exercise of a unique guile and persistence, and would continue to survive, unknown and disregarded, long after the motorways had collapsed into dust.

Parts of the island dated from well before World War II. The eastern end, below the overpass, was its oldest section, with the churchyard and the ground-courses of Edwardian terraced houses. The breaker's yard and its wrecked cars had been superimposed on the still identifiable streets and alleyways.

In the centre of the island were the air-raid shelters among which he was sitting. Attached to these was a later addition, the remains of a Civil Defence post little more than fifteen years old. Maitland climbed down from the shelter. Supported by the grass blades swirling around him like a flock of eager attendants, he hobbled westwards down the centre of the island. He crossed a succession of low walls, partly buried under piles of discarded tyres and worn steel cable.

Around the ruin of a former paybox, Maitland identified the ground-plan of a post-war cinema, a narrow single-storey flea pit built from cement blocks and galvanized iron. Ten feet away, partly screened by a bank of nettles, steps ran down to a basement.

Looking at the shuttered paybox, Maitland thought unclearly of his own childhood visits to the local cinema, with its endless pro-

grammes of vampire and horror movies. More and more, the island was becoming an exact model of his head. His movement
across this forgotten terrain was a journey not merely through the
island's past but through his own. His infantile anger as he shouted
aloud for Catherine reminded him of how, as a child, he had once
bellowed unwearyingly for his mother while she nursed his younger
sister in the next room. For some reason, which he had always resented, she had never come to pacify him, but had let him climb
from the empty bath himself, hoarse with anger and surprise.

Too exhausted to press on, Maitland sat on a stone wall. Around
him the high nettles rose into the sunlight, their tiered and serrated
leaves like the towers of Gothic cathedrals, or the porous rocks of
a mineral forest on an alien planet. Hunger contracted his stomach in a sudden spasm, forcing him to vomit on to his knees. He
wiped away the phlegm and hobbled across the brick courses to the
southern embankment.

Losing consciousness for short intervals, he wandered to and
fro, his eyes unfocused, following the blunted end of the crutch.

As he tottered about, Maitland found himself losing interest in
his own body, and in the pain that inflamed his leg. He began to
shuck off sections of his body, forgetting first his injured hip, then
both his legs, erasing all awareness of his bruised chest and dia-
phragm. Sustained by the cold air, he moved through the grass,
looking round calmly at those features of the island he had come
to know so well during the past days. Identifying the island with
himself, he gazed at the cars in the breaker's yard, at the wire-mesh
fence, and the concrete caisson behind him. These places of pain
and ordeal were now confused with pieces of his body. He gestured
towards them, trying to make a circuit of the island so that he could
leave these sections of himself where they belonged. He would leave

his right leg at the point of his crash, his bruised hands impaled upon the steel fence. He would place his chest where he had sat against the concrete wall. At each point a small ritual would signify the transfer of obligation from himself to the island.

He spoke aloud, a priest officiating at the eucharist of his own body.

'I am the island.'

The air shed its light.

10

the air-raid shelter

Traffic drummed above his head. Smoke rose from a cigarette butt tossed into the grass a few feet from his face. Maitland watched the smoke entwine itself through the tall blades, which leaned towards him, swaying in the late afternoon sunlight as if urging him to his feet. He sat up, trying to clear his mind. The fever had soaked his body, burning the raw skin beneath his beard.

On all sides of the island the traffic moved along the motorways. Steadying himself, Maitland fixed his eyes on the distant cars. He climbed to his feet, hanging himself from the crutch like a carcass on a butcher's hook. High above him, the illuminated surface of the route indicator shone like a burning sword in the dark sky.

Maitland found a last rubber marker in his jacket pocket. On the drying concrete he scrawled:

CATHERINE HELP TOO FAST

The letters wound up and down the slope. Maitland concentrated on the spelling, but ten minutes later, when he returned after an unsuccessful attempt to reach the Jaguar, they had been rubbed out as if by some dissatisfied examiner.

MOTHER DONT HURT POLICE

He waited in the long grass beside the embankment, but his eyes closed. When he opened them, the message had vanished.

He gave up, unable to decipher his own writing. The grass swayed reassuringly, beckoning this fever-racked scarecrow into its interior. The blades swirled around him, opening a dozen pathways, each of which would carry him to some paradisial arbour. Knowing that unless he reached the shelter of the Jaguar he would not survive the night, Maitland set his course for the breaker's yard, but after a few minutes he followed the grass passively as it wove its spiral patterns around him.

To his surprise, it carried him up a slope of steeper and more difficult ground, over the roof of the largest of the air-raid shelters. Maitland laboured along, listening to the grass seethe around him. A stony ridge marked the west wall of the shelter. Maitland paused there. The curving roof fell away on either side, disappearing into the dense undergrowth that sprang from the floor of the pit.

The grass was silent now, as if waiting for Maitland to make some significant move. Wondering why he had climbed on to the shelter, Maitland caught sight of the overturned taxi in the breaker's yard. He turned with his last strength to reach the Jaguar. Before he could catch himself he slipped on the rain-damp roof. He fell heavily, and slid down the rounded slope into the grass and nettles, plunging through them like a diver vanishing into the deeps of an underground cavern.

Submerged in this green bower, Maitland lay for some time in a hammock of crushed nettles. The dense grass and the foliage of a stunted elder sealed off all but a faint glow of the late afternoon sunlight, and he could almost believe that he was lying at the bottom of a calm and peaceful sea, through which a few bars of faint light penetrated the pelagic quiet. This silence and the reassuring organic smell of decaying vegetation soothed his fever.

A small, sharp-footed creature moved across his left leg, its claws clutching for purchase in the worn fabric of his trousers. It darted in brief scurries, reaching up his thigh to his groin. Opening his eyes, Maitland peered through the dim light, recognizing the long muzzle and nervous eyes of a brown rat drawn to him by the scent of the blood leaking from his hip. An open wound disfigured the creature's head, exposing the skull, as if it had recently torn itself from a trap.

'Get out—aah!' Maitland leapt forward, seizing the metal crutch in the elder branches above his head. He thrashed wildly at the foliage, beating back the walls of his green cell.

The rat had gone. Maitland forced his left leg through the branches to the ground below and stepped out into the fading evening light. He was standing in a sunken passage that ran along the western wall of the shelter. Here the vegetation had been cut back, forming a rough slope that ran down the bank to the doorway of the shelter.

'Tools . . . !'

Fumbling excitedly with the crutch, Maitland lurched down the passage, his fever and injured leg forgotten. When he reached the door he wiped away the sweat that soaked his face and forehead. A chromium padlock and chain locked the door. Maitland forced the crutch inside the chain and jerked it from its mountings.

Kicking back the door, Maitland hobbled forward into the shelter. A sweet but not unpleasant smell greeted him, as if he were stepping into the lair of some large and docile creature. In the fading light he could see that the shelter was an abandoned beggar's hovel. A line of faded quilts hung from the ceiling and covered the walls and floor. A pile of blankets formed a small bed, and the sole pieces of furniture were a wooden chair and table. From the back of the chair hung a ragged leotard, the faded costume of some pre-war circus acrobat.

Maitland leaned against the curving wall, deciding that he would pass the night in this deserted lair. On the wooden table a number of metal objects were arranged in a circle like ornaments on an altar. All had been taken from motorcar bodies—a wing mirror, strips of chromium window trim, pieces of broken headlamp.

'Jaguar . . . ?' Maitland recognized the manufacturer's medallion, of the same type as that on his own car.

As he picked up the medallion to examine it he was unaware of the broad, thick chested figure who was watching him from the doorway, head lowered like a bull's between swaying shoulders.

Before Maitland could raise the medallion to the light a heavy fist knocked it from his hands. The crutch was snatched away and flung into the open air. Powerful hands seized him by the arms and hurled him backwards through the door. During the next seconds, as he was flung to the ground, Maitland was only aware of the panting, bull-like figure dragging him up the slope into the last light of the day. The headlamps of the distant traffic moved with an almost dream-like calm as the man's face gasped into his own, gusting out a hot breath of rancid wine. Slapping Maitland with his fists, his attacker rolled him backwards and forwards across the damp ground, grunting to himself as if trying to discover some secret hidden on Maitland's injured body.

As he lost consciousness Maitland caught a last glimpse of the passing traffic on the motorway. Between his attacker's swinging arms he saw a red-haired young woman in a camouflage-patterned combat jacket running towards them with the metal crutch lifted in her strong hands.

11

rescue

'Rest—try not to move. We've sent for help.'

The young woman's quiet voice soothed Maitland. Her hands bathed his face with a tampon of cotton wool. He lay back as the hot water stung his bruised skin, aware of the fever burning through his bones. As the young woman lifted his head the water trickled through his beard. He opened his swollen mouth, trying to catch the scalding drops.

'I'll give you a drink—you must be thirsty.'

She gestured with her elbow at the plastic mug standing on the packing case beside the bed, but made no effort to pass it to Maitland. Her firm hands moved around his neck and down to his chest. Maitland was no longer wearing the dinner jacket, and the damp dress shirt was black with oil.

An unshaded paraffin lamp standing on the floor by the doorway glared into his eyes when he tried to look at the young woman's face. As he stirred fretfully, aware of the pain in his leg, she drew the red blanket around his shoulders.

'Relax, Mr Maitland. We've called for help. Catherine—is that your wife's name?'

Maitland nodded weakly. He felt numbed by his relief at being rescued. When she placed her left arm under his head and lifted the mug to his mouth he could smell her warm, strong body, a medley of scents and odours that made his mind reel.

He was lying in a small room, little more than ten feet by ten and almost filled by the metal double bed and mattress on which he was lying. A blocked-off ventilation shaft rose from the centre of the ceiling, but the room was windowless. Beyond the open doorway a flight of semicircular steps led to the floor above. A faded cinema poster hung from the wall at the foot of the bed, advertising a Ginger Rogers and Fred Astaire musical. On either side were several more up-to-date prints taken from underground magazines—a psychedelic poster in the Beardsley manner, a grainy close-up of the dead Che Guevara, a Black Power manifesto, and Charles Manson at his trial, psychotic eyes staring out beneath a bald skull. Apart from the packing case beside the bed the only piece of furniture in the room was a card table stacked with cosmetic jars and scent bottles, mascara sticks and scruffed-up tissues. An expensive leather suitcase was propped against the wall. A skirt and sweater, and various pieces of underwear, were strung on hangers from the lid.

Maitland gathered himself together. The fever had begun to subside. He remembered the violent attack in the air-raid shelter, and being dragged into the open evening air, but the pain of these blows had been dissolved by the young woman's first words. In the context of his ordeal on the island even this shabby room—in a decaying neighbourhood somewhere near the motorway, he assumed—took on all the style and comfort of a riverside suite at the Savoy. As the young woman sat down on the bed he took her hand, trying to express his gratitude to her.

'Are we . . .' he began through his bruised mouth. 'Are we near the island?' He added, realizing that she might not be aware of this, 'I crashed my car . . . Jaguar . . . I went off the motorway.'

The young woman chewed pensively on a stick of gum, watching Maitland with her sharp eyes.

'Yes, we know. You're lucky that you're still alive.' She placed her strong hand on his forehead, feeling his temperature. 'Were you ill before the crash? You've got quite a fever, you know.'

Maitland shook his head, glad to feel the pressure of her cool palm. 'No—it started later. Yesterday, I think. My leg . . . it's broken.'

'Good. I thought so. Poor man, I'll give you something to eat.'

As Maitland waited, she reached into her handbag and took out a bar of milk chocolate. She peeled back the silver foil, broke off several of the squares and placed the first one between Maitland's lips.

While the warm chocolate dissolved in his mouth, Maitland was able to see the young woman's face for the first time. She stood up and peered at herself in the travelling mirror hanging from the wall. Bar of chocolate in one hand, she paced up and down the narrow floor. Lit by the paraffin lamp behind her, her red hair glowed like a wild sun in the shabby room, shafts of light cutting through the home-set waves that rose above her high forehead. She was about twenty, with an angular, sharp-witted face and strong jaw. She was good-looking in an almost wilfully tatty way. Her manner towards Maitland, as she fed the soft chocolate to him, each square finger-printed by her thumb, was brusque and deferential at the same time. Possibly she resented having to look after this well-to-do man who had been brought to her meagre room, realizing that he would soon leave for surroundings that were very much more comfortable. Yet something about her tone, the confident intonations of her voice, suggested to Maitland that she had come from a rather different background. With her faded jeans and combat jacket, surrounded by the Manson and Black Power posters, she looked like the prototypal dropout, but this impression in turn was belied by the mass of cheap cosmetics, the tarty hairdo and garish clothes hanging from the suitcase lid, the make-believe equipment of a street walker.

Revived by the water and chocolate, Maitland massaged his mouth with one hand. At any moment the ambulance attendants would arrive, he would be carried away to a hospital bed in Hammersmith.

'You called the ambulance? They'll be coming soon. I'd like to thank you . . . ?'

'Jane—Jane Sheppard. I haven't done very much.'

'I've almost forgotten how to eat. There's another number I want you to ring. Dr Helen Fairfax—do you mind?'

'No—but I'm not on the phone. Try to relax. You're absolutely exhausted.'

She sat on the bed, exploring his right hip with her firm fingers. She grimaced as she peered at the inflamed wound exposed through the rent in his trousers. 'This looks nasty. I'll try to clean it for you.'

Her hands moved around his hips and groin as she tried to losen his trousers. The chocolate melting in Maitland's stomach made him feel light-headed. 'It's all right. They'll deal with it at the hospital.'

He began to tell the young woman about his crash, eager to fix his nightmare ordeal in someone else's mind before it vanished.

'I was trapped there for three days—it's hard to believe now. My car went over the edge, I don't think I was hurt at first. But I couldn't get off. Nobody stopped! It's amazing—I was starving to death on this traffic island. Unless you'd come I would have died there . . .'

Maitland broke off. Jane Sheppard was sitting with her back to him, her hip pressing against his right elbow. Her hands worked away expertly at his trousers. She had extended the slit to the waistband, but the rubberized fabric was too strong for the pair of nail-scissors in her hand. Lifting his right buttock, she began to cut at the lining of his hip pocket.

Maitland watched her remove his car keys from the pocket. She looked hard at them, turning over each of the three keys, and caught his eye. With a small laugh she put them on the packing case.

'You were uncomfortable . . .' As if to make the explanation convincing, she slid her hand on to his buttock and massaged the bruised skin for a few seconds.

'So no one stopped? I suppose you were surprised. These days we don't notice other people's selfishness until we're on the receiving end ourselves.'

Maitland turned his head, his eyes meeting her level gaze. He stopped himself from picking up the keys. His sense of relief and exhilaration had begun to fade, and he looked around the room, establishing its reality in his mind. Part of himself was still lying out in the rain, listening to the invisible, endlessly drumming traffic. For a moment he was frightened that the room and its young tenant might be part of some terminal delusion.

'It's kind of you to look after me. You have called the ambulance?'

'I've arranged for help, yes. A friend of mine has gone. You'll be all right.'

'Where are we exactly—are we near the island?'

'The "island"—is that what you call it?'

'The traffic island. The patch of waste ground below the motorway. Are we near there?'

'We're near the motorway, yes. You're quite safe, Mr Maitland.'

Maitland listened to the distant murmur of the traffic. He noticed that his wristwatch had gone, but he guessed it to be somewhere near midnight—hard experience told him that the last westbound traffic was leaving central London.

'My watch must have fallen off. How do you know my name?'

'We found some papers, in a briefcase near the car. Anyway, you talk to yourself all the time.' She paused, eyeing him critically. 'You're tremendously angry with yourself about something, aren't you?'

Maitland ignored this. 'You've seen the car? The silver Jaguar?'

'No—I mean, yes, I did. You confuse me when you talk about the island all the time.' Half-resentfully, as if reminding Maitland of his debt to her, she said, 'I brought you here. You're damned heavy, you know, even for a big man.'

'Where are we—the traffic . . .' Alarmed, Maitland tried to sit up. The young woman stood at the foot of the bed, her red hair inflamed by the paraffin lamp. She stared at Maitland like a down-at-heel witch who by some confused alchemy had conjured an over-large victim into her lair and was unsure how best to exploit the possibilities of the cadaver.

Unsettled by her calm gaze, Maitland glanced around the room. In one corner, supporting a metal basin filled with wet underwear, were three circular cans, each the size of a film reel.

Projecting like horns from the wall behind the girl's head were the brackets of some kind of winding device. Maitland looked up at the ventilator shaft, and at the Astaire and Rogers publicity poster.

j. g. ballard

Jane Sheppard spoke quietly. 'Go on. What is it? You're obviously straining to realize something.'

'The cinema . . .' Maitland pointed to the ceiling. 'Of course, the basement of the ruined cinema.' He lowered his head wearily on to the stale pillow. 'My God, I'm still on the island . . .'

'Stop talking about the island! You can leave any time you want, I'm not keeping you here. It may not be good enough for you, but I've done what I can. If it hadn't been for me you wouldn't be around any more to complain!'

Maitland brought a hand to his face, feeling the sweat pour from his skin. 'Oh my God . . . Look—I need a doctor.'

'We'll call a doctor. You must rest now. You've been overexciting yourself for days, deliberately, I think.'

'Jane, I'll give you some money. Help me up on to the road and stop a car. How much money do you want?'

Jane stopped pacing up and down the room. She looked back cannily at Maitland. 'Have you got any money?'

Maitland nodded wearily. Communicating the simplest information seemed to tax this intelligent but devious woman. Clearly she suspected everything around her.

'Yes—I'm well off . . . a senior partner in a firm of architects. You'll be paid all you want, without any questions. Now, have you sent for help?'

Jane ignored this. 'Have you any money here—say five pounds?'

'In my wallet—it's in my car, in the trunk. I've got about thirty pounds. I'll give you ten.'

'In the trunk . . .' Jane pondered this, and with a deft movement of her hand picked up the keys. 'I'd better look after these.'

Too tired to move, Maitland stared at the Charles Manson poster. Again he found himself losing the will to survive. He needed

to sleep on the warm bed with its smell of cheap scent, in this windowless room deep in the ground. Far above, he heard the grass
seething in the night wind.

Heavy boots clattered down the staircase, barely waking him.
Jane stepped forward aggressively. Deferring to her, the visitor stood
outside the door, a scarred hand shielding his small eyes from the
paraffin lamp. As he panted from the exertion of moving his burly
body down the steps, Maitland recognized the harsh, phlegmy
breathing of the man who had attacked him.

The man was about fifty years old, plainly a mental defective
of some kind, his low forehead blunted by a lifetime of uncer-
tainty. His puckered face had the expression of a puzzled child,
as if whatever limited intelligence he had been born with had never
developed beyond his adolescence. All the stresses of a hard life
had combined to produce this aged defective, knocked about by a
race of unkind and indifferent adults but still clinging to his in-
nocent faith in a simple world.

Ridges of silver scar tissue marked his cheeks and eyebrows,
almost joining across the depressed bridge of his nose, a blob of
amorphous cartilage that needed endless attention. He wiped it
with his strong hand, examining the phlegm in the paraffin light.
Though clumsy, his body still had a certain power and athletic
poise. As he swayed from side to side on his small feet Maitland
saw that he moved with the marred grace of an acrobat or punch-
drunk sparring partner who had gone down the hard way. He con-
tinually touched his face, like a boxer flicking away the sting of a
sharp blow.

'Well, Proctor, did you find them?' Jane asked.

The man shook his head. He bounced from one foot to the next
like a child too busy to visit the lavatory.

'Locked,' he announced in a gruff voice. 'Too strong for Proctor.'

'I'm surprised—I thought you could break anything. We'll look again tomorrow, in the daylight.'

'Yes—Proctor find them tomorrow.' He peered over her shoulder at Maitland, and she stepped back reluctantly.

'Proctor, he's nearly asleep. Don't wake him, or we'll have a corpse on our hands.'

'No, Miss Jane.'

Proctor stepped forward with exaggerated caution. Maitland turned his head, realizing that the man was wearing his dinner jacket. The silk lapels gleamed as they were bunched outwards by the tight fit.

Jane had also noticed the garment.

'What the hell are you wearing that for?' she asked sharply. 'Are you going to a party, or just dressing for dinner?'

Proctor giggled at this. He looked down at himself, not without dignity. 'To a party. Yes . . . Proctor and Miss Jane!'

'God Almighty . . . Well, take it off.'

Proctor gazed incredulously at her, his broken face in an expression of pleading and resentment. He clung to the points of the lapels, as if frightened that they would fly away.

'Proctor! Do you want to be seen straight away? They'll spot you a mile off in that fancy dress!'

Proctor hovered in the doorway, accepting the logic of this but reluctant to part with the jacket.

'Night only,' he temporized. 'At night no one will see Proctor's jacket.'

'All right—at night only. Don't let it go to your head, though.'

She pointed to Maitland, who lay half-asleep on the damp pillow. 'I'm going out, so you'll have to keep an eye on him. Just leave him alone. Don't start fiddling around with him, or hitting him again. And I don't want you in this room—sit at the top of the steps.'

Proctor nodded obediently. Like an eager conspirator, he sidled backwards through the door and climbed the staircase. Woken by the clatter on the wooden steps, Maitland recognized the industrial boots whose prints he had seen on the embankment. He tried to rouse himself, frightened of being left alone with this punch-drunk resident of the island. He assumed now that the tramp had scaled the muddy slope and replaced the trestles, hiding all traces of his accident.

As he muttered to the young woman she sat down on the bed beside him. A sweet, euphoric smoke filled the room, hanging in long decks around her face. She cradled Maitland's head with un-expected gentleness.

For five minutes she comforted Maitland, rocking his head and murmuring to him reassuringly.

'You'll be all right, love. Try to sleep, you'll feel better when you wake. I'll look after you, dear. You're sleepy, aren't you, my baby? Poor bundle, you need so much sleep. Sleepy baby, my rock-a-bye babe . . .'

When she had gone, Maitland lay half-awake in his fever, conscious of the tramp in his dinner jacket watching him from the doorway. All night Proctor hovered over him, his heavy fingers roving around Maitland's body, as if searching for some talisman that eluded him. Now and then Maitland would smell the hot breath of rancid wine in his mouth, and wake to see Proctor's broken face staring down at him. In the light of the paraffin lamp his scarred face seemed to be made of polished stone.

A few hours before dawn Jane Sheppard returned. Maitland heard her calling out in the distance as she crossed the island. She dismissed Proctor, who disappeared silently into the seething grass.

There was a clatter of high-heeled shoes down the steps. Maitland watched her passively when she lurched across to the bed. Slightly drunk, she gazed down at Maitland as if not recognizing him.

'God—are you still here? I thought you were going. What a hell of an evening.'

Crooning to herself, she kicked away her stiletto-heeled shoes. Where she had been he could only guess from her costume, a caricature of a small-town forties whore—a divided skirt that revealed her thighs and stocking tops, pointed breasts under a Day-Glo blouse.

She tottered round to the far side of the bed and undressed, heaving the clothes into the suitcase. When she was naked she slipped under the frayed blanket. She stared up at the Rogers and Astaire poster and took Maitland's hand in her own, partly to still him, partly for company. During the remainder of the night and early morning, as he lay beside her, Maitland was aware in his fever of her strong body touching his own.

12

the acrobat

The next morning Jane Sheppard had gone. When Maitland woke
the basement room was silent. A shaft of sunlight down the narrow staircase illuminated the shabby bed on which he lay. The faces
of Guevara and Charles Manson hung from the walls, presiding
over him like the custodians of a nightmare.

Maitland reached out his hand, feeling the imprint of the young
woman's body. Still lying there, he looked around the room, taking
in the open suitcase, the gaudy dresses on their hangers, the cosmetics on the card table. Jane had straightened everything before
leaving.

His fever had subsided. Maitland picked up the plastic cup on
the packing case, lifted himself on to one elbow and drank the tepid
water. He pulled back the blankets and examined his leg. Some
wayward healing process had locked the hip joint into its socket,
but the swelling and pain had eased. For the first time he was able
to touch the bruised flesh.

Maitland sat quietly on the edge of the bed, staring at the

Astaire and Rogers poster. He tried to remember if he had ever seen the film, casting his mind back to his adolescence. For several successive years he had devoured almost the whole of Hollywood's output, sitting alone in the empty circles of huge suburban Odeons. He massaged his bruised chest, realizing that his body was more and more beginning to resemble that of his younger self— the combination of hunger and fever had made him lose at least ten pounds in weight. His broad chest and heavy legs had shed half their muscle.

Maitland slid the injured leg on to the floor and listened to the traffic sounds from the motorway. The certainty that he would soon be leaving the island revived him. He had now been marooned on this triangle of waste ground for almost four days. He knew that he had begun to forget his wife and son, Helen Fairfax and his partners—together they had moved back into the dimmer light at the rear of his mind, their places taken by the urgencies of food, shelter, his injured leg and, above all, the need to dominate the patch of ground immediately around him. His effective horizon had shrunk to little more than ten feet away. Even though he would escape in under an hour—however reluctantly, the young woman and Proctor would help him up the embankment—the prospect obsessed him like some decade-long quest.

'Damned leg . . .'

Inside the packing case were a primus stove and an unwashed saucepan. Maitland scraped the brown crust of dry rice from the pan, hungrily forcing the hard grains into his bruised mouth. A thick beard covered his face—he looked down at the grimy dress-shirt, the blackened trousers slit from the right knee to the waist-band. Yet this collection of tatters less and less resembled an eccentric costume.

Leaning against the wall, Maitland swung himself around the room. The Guevara poster tore in his hands and hung swaying from a corner pin. He reached the doorway, turned himself on his good leg and sat on the lid of a fifty-gallon drum that served as a water butt.

A dozen steps led up to the bright sunlight. From the steep angle of the sun Maitland guessed that it was about eleven thirty. The quiet Sunday-morning traffic moved along the motorway—within half an hour or so some good-humoured family out for a day's drive would be startled by a haggard man in ragged evening dress staggering across the road in front of them. The longest hangover in the world.

Maitland moved up the steps towards the sunlight. When he reached the top he lifted his head cautiously, peering through the grass and nettles that surrounded the stairwell.

He was about to step on to the island when he heard a familiar phlegmy breathing. Maitland crouched down, and eased himself across the ground to the derelict paybox. Lying on his side, he reached out and parted a bank of nettles with his arms.

Twenty feet away, in a small hollow surrounded by the nettles and high grass, Proctor was performing a set of gymnastic exercises. Blowing hard through his mouth, he stood with his bare feet together, strong shoulders braced as he raised his arms in front of himself. A skipping rope and the steel-capped boots were parked on the well-worn ground of this private recreation yard. He was dressed in the ragged remains of the circus leotard which Maitland had seen hanging from a chair in the air-raid shelter. The silver strips showed off his powerful shoulders, and revealed the livid scar that ran like a lightning bolt from the back of his right ear down his neck to his shoulder, the residue of some appalling act of violence.

After preparing himself, an elaborate ritual of puffing and pant-ing like the start-up of an old gas engine, Proctor took a short step forward and leapt into a somersault. His powerful body whirled in the air. He struck the ground heavily, barely holding his balance, legs bent and arms wavering at his sides. Delighted by this triumph, he stamped happily in his bare feet.

Maitland waited as Proctor prepared for his next feat. From the careful buildup, the repeated pacing about and measuring of him-self against the air, it was clear that this next acrobatic turn repre-sented his real test. Proctor concentrated all his energies. He marked out the ground, kicking away the loose stones like a large animal searching for the kindest terrain. When he finally leaped again into the air, attempting a backward somersault, Maitland al-ready knew that he would fail. He lowered his head as the tramp sprawled across the ground, scattering his boots.

Stunned, Proctor lay on his back. He picked himself up, look-ing dejectedly at his clumsy body. He made a half-hearted attempt to prepare himself for a second attempt, but gave up and brushed the dust from his grazed arms. He had cut his right wrist. He sucked at the wound, and tried a handstand, following it with a crude knee fall. His coordination was clearly at fault, and the for-ward somersault had come off by chance alone. Even skipping was too much for him. Within seconds the rope was tangled around his neck.

Nevertheless, as Maitland realized, the tramp was not dismayed. He licked the cut on his wrist and panted happily to himself, more than satisfied with his progress. Embarrassed by the display, Mait-land edged away.

Hearing Maitland move behind the paybox, Proctor turned

suspiciously. Before Maitland could reach the staircase he had disappeared from sight, vanishing like a startled animal into the deep
grass.

There was a faint movement in the nettle bank behind Maitland.
He waited, certain that Proctor was watching him and that if he
stepped out the tramp would seize him and hurl him back down
the steps. Maitland listened to the traffic, thinking of the tramp's
unconcealed strain of violence, a long-borne hostility to the intelligent world on which he would happily revenge himself.

Maitland eased himself down the steps. From the bottom of the
stairwell he looked up at the sky and the waving grass. He stepped
back into the room and swung himself around the walls. As his eyes
cleared in the dim light he gazed round at the underground posters, the dingy bed and leather suitcase filled with cheap clothes.
Who were these two tenants of the island? What uneasy alliance
existed between the old circus hand and this sharp-witted young
woman? She appeared to be a classic drop-out, exiting from a well-
to-do family with her head full of half-baked ideals, on the run from
the police for a drug or probation offence.

Maitland heard her voice call out across the deep grass. Proctor answered in his gruff simpleton's tones. Maitland moved back
to the bed and lay down, covering himself with the blanket as Jane
came down the steps into the room.

In one hand was a supermarket bag filled with groceries. She
was wearing her jeans and combat jacket. For once, Maitland reflected as he noticed the mud on her shoes, the camouflage was not
merely a youthful fad. Presumably she knew some private route up
the embankment and across the feeder road.

She peered at Maitland, her sharp eyes taking in everything in a one-second glance. Her red hair was brushed back tightly against her head like a hard-working mill-girl's, exposing her high, bony forehead.

'How are you? Not too strong, I imagine. Anyway, you slept well.'

Maitland gestured weakly with one hand. Something warned him to disguise his recovery. 'I feel a little better.'

'I see you've been wandering around in here,' she remarked without any criticism. She straightened the Guevara poster, re-pinning the torn corner. 'You can't be too bad. There's nothing to find here, by the way.'

She put her strong hand to Maitland's forehead and held it there, then briskly pulled out the primus stove and carried it into the sunlight at the bottom of the stairwell.

'Your fever's gone. We were worried about you last night. You're the sort of man who has to test himself all the time. Do you think you crashed on to this traffic island deliberately?' When Maitland regarded her patiently she went on, 'I'm not joking—believe me, self-destruction is something I know all about. My mother pumped herself so full of barbiturates before she died that she turned blue.'

She lit the primus and set three eggs boiling in the pan. 'You must be hungry—I bought some things for you at the supermarket.'

Maitland sat up. 'What day is it?'

'Sunday—the Indian places around here are open every day. They exploit themselves and their staffs more than the white owners do. But that's something you know all about.'

'What's that?'

'Exploitation. You're a rich businessman, aren't you? That's what you claimed to be last night.'

'Jane, you've being naïve—I'm not rich and I'm not a businessman. I'm an architect.' Maitland paused, well aware of the way in which she was reducing their relationship to the level of this aimless domestic banter. Yet there was something not entirely calculated about this.

'Did you call for help?' he asked firmly.

Jane ignored the question, setting out the modest meal. The brightly coloured paper cups and plates, and the paper table cloth she spread carefully across the packing case, made it resemble a miniature children's tea party.

'I . . . didn't have time. I thought you needed some food first.'

'As a matter of fact, I'm starving.' Maitland unwrapped the packet of rusks she handed to him. 'But I've got to get to a hospital. My leg needs looking at. There's the office, and my wife—they must wonder where I am.'

'But they think you're away on a business trip,' Jane retorted quickly. 'They probably aren't missing you at all.'

Maitland let this pass. 'You told me you'd called the police last night.'

Jane laughed at Maitland as he hunched in his ragged clothes on the edge of the bed, his blackened hands tearing apart the packet of rusks. 'Not the police—we're not very fond of them here. Proctor isn't, anyway—he has rather unhappy memories of the police. They've always kicked him around. Do you know that a sergeant from Notting Hill Station urinated on him? You don't forget that kind of thing.'

She waited for a reply. The sulphurous smell of the cracked eggs intoxicated Maitland. She steered a steaming egg on to his paper plate, leaning across him long enough for him to register the weight and body of her left breast. 'Look, you weren't well last night. You couldn't have been moved. That terrible leg, the fever, you were completely exhausted, raving away about your wife. Can you imagine us stumbling about in the dark, trying to carry you up that slope? I just wanted to keep you alive.'

Maitland broke the boiled egg. The hot shell stung the oil-filled cuts in his fingers. The young woman squatted on the floor at his feet, shaking out her red hair. The contrived way in which she used her body confused him.

'You'll help me afterwards to get away from here,' he told her. 'I understand your not wanting the police involved. If Proctor . . .'

'Exactly. He's terrified of the police, he'll do anything to avoid bringing them here. It's not that he's ever done anything, but this place is all he's got. When they built the motorway they sealed him in—he never leaves here, you know. It's pretty remarkable how he's survived.'

Maitland crammed the dripping fragments of the egg into his mouth. 'He nearly killed me,' he commented, licking his fingers.

'He thought you were trying to take over his den. It was lucky I came along. He's very strong. When he was sixteen or seventeen he used to be a trapeze artist with some fly-by-night circus. That was before they had any safety legislation. He fell off the high wire and damaged his brain. They just threw him out. Mental defectives and subnormals are treated appallingly—unless they're prepared to go into institutions they have absolutely no protection.'

Maitland nodded, concentrating on the food. 'How long have you been in this old cinema?'

'I don't really live here,' she answered with a flourish. 'I'm staying with some . . . friends, near the Harrow Road. I used to have my own study as a child, I don't like too many people around me—you probably understand.'

'Jane—' Maitland cleared his throat. Eating the hard rusks and scalding egg had opened a dozen sore places in his mouth. His gums and lips, the soft palate, stung from the unaccustomed bite. He looked down unsteadily at the young woman, realizing the extent of his dependence on her. Seventy yards away the traffic moved along the motorway, carrying people to their family lunches. Sitting over a primus stove with her in this shabby room for some reason reminded him of the first months of his marriage to Catherine, and their formal meals. Although Catherine had furnished the apartment herself, virtually without consulting Maitland, he had felt the same dependence on her, the same satisfaction at being surrounded by strange furniture. Even their present house had been designed to avoid the hazards of overfamiliarity.

He realized that Jane had spoken the truth about saving his life, and felt a sudden debt to her. He was puzzled by her mixture of warmth and aggression, her swerves from blunt speaking to outright deviousness. More and more, he found himself looking at her body, and was irritated by his own sexual response to the offhand way in which she exploited herself.

'Jane, I want you to call Proctor now. You and he can carry me up the embankment and leave me there. I'll be able to stop a driver.'

'Of course.' She looked frankly into his eyes, giving him a small smile. A hand stroked the hair behind her neck. 'Proctor won't help you, but I'll try—you're awfully heavy, even if you have been starving. Too many expense-account lunches, terrible tax evasion goes on. Still, you're supposed to get some kind of emotional security from overeating . . .'

'Jane!' Exasperated, Maitland drummed with his blackened fist on the packing case, scattering the paper plates on to the floor. 'I'm not going to call the police. I won't report either you or Proctor.

I'm grateful to you—if you hadn't found me I would probably have died here. No one will find out.'

Jane shrugged, already losing interest in what Maitland was saying. 'People *will* come . . .'

'They won't! The breakdown men who tow my car away won't give a damn about anything here. The last three days have proved that to me a hundred times over.'

'Is your car worth a lot of money?'

'No—it's a write-off. I set fire to it.'

'I know. We watched that. Why not leave it here?'

'The insurance people will want to see it.' Maitland looked at her sharply. 'You *saw* the fire? Good God, why didn't you help me then?'

'We didn't know who you were. How much did the car cost?'

Maitland gazed into her open and childlike face, with its expression of naïve corruption.

'Is that it? Is that why you're in no hurry to see me go?' He put a hand reassuringly on her shoulder, holding it there when she tried to push it away. 'Jane, listen to me. If you want money I'll give it to you. Now, how much do you want?'

Her question was as matter-of-fact as a bored cashier's. 'Have you got any money?'

'Yes, I have—in the bank. There's my wallet in the car, with about thirty pounds in it. You've got the keys, get there before Proctor does. You look fast enough on your feet.'

Ignoring his hostility, she reached into her handbag. After a pause she took out the oil-stained wallet. She tossed it on to the bed beside Maitland.

'It's all there—count it. Go on! *Count* it!'

Maitland opened the wallet and glanced at the bundle of damp notes. Calming himself, he started again.

'Jane, I can help you. What do you want?'

'Nothing from you.' She had found a piece of gum and was chewing on it aggressively. 'You're the one who needs help. You were screwed up by being on your own too much. Let's face it, you're not really unhappy with your wife. You like that cool scene.'

Maitland waited for her to finish. 'All right, maybe I do. Then help me get away from here.'

She stood in front of him, blocking his path to the door, eyes furious.

'You're making these assumptions all the time! No one owes you anything, so stop all this want, want, want! You crashed your car because you drove too fast, now you're complaining about it like a child. We only found you last night . . .'

Maitland avoided her fierce gaze, and pulled himself along the wall to the doorway. This deranged young woman needed someone to be angry with—the old tramp was too dim, but he himself, starving and half-crippled by a broken leg, made the perfect target. The first show of gratitude was enough to set her going . . .

As he passed her she stepped forward and took his arm. She slipped it around her small shoulders. Like a dance-hall instructress leading a helpless novice, she steered him towards the stairs.

Maitland stepped into the bright sunlight. The long grass seethed around his legs, greeting him like an affectionate dog. Fed by the spring rain, the grass was over four feet deep, reaching to Maitland's chest. He leaned unsteadily against the young woman. The high causeway of the overpass spanned the air a hundred yards to the east, and he could see the concrete caisson on which he had

scrawled his messages. The island seemed larger and more con-
toured, a labyrinth of dips and hollows. The vegetation was wild
and lush, as if the island was moving back in time to an earlier and
more violent period.

'The messages I wrote—did you wipe them off?'

'Proctor did. He never learned to read and write. He hates words
of any kind.'

'And the wooden trestles?' Maitland felt no resentment towards
either Proctor or the young woman.

'He straightened them—right after the crash, while you were
still stunned in the car.'

She supported him, standing against his shoulder, one hand
pressed against his stomach. The scent of her warm body contrasted
with the smell of the grass and the automobile exhaust gases. Maitland sat down on a truck tyre lying on the ground. He gazed at
the high wall of the motorway embankment. The newly seeded
grass was growing more densely on the surface. Soon it would
hide all traces of his accident, the deep ruts left by the tyres of his
car, the confused marks of his first struggles to climb the embankment. Maitland felt a brief moment of regret that he was leaving
the island. He would have liked to preserve it for ever, so that he
could bring Catherine and his friends to see this place of ordeal.

'Jane . . .'

The young woman had gone. Twenty yards away, her strong
head and shoulders moved above the grass as she strode towards
the air raid shelters.

13

the fire signal

'Jane! Come here . . . *Jane!*

His weak voice, almost a scold, faded into the seething grass. Maitland stood up and swung himself after her, hopping on his left leg. Choking with anger, he leaned against the shuttered paybox. As he calmed himself he massaged his stomach, feeling the hard edge of his rib cage. At least he had received some food from the girl.

Fifteen feet from him, on the roof of a ruined outhouse, was a rusty metal pipe, one end bend into a crude handle. The crutch! Maitland hobbled across the stony ground, dragging his injured leg after him. His long arms hauled his body over the broken brick-work of the outhouse. He reached up and seized the exhaust pipe.

Sitting with it in his hands, he caught his breath. He waved the crutch at the passing cars, glad to feel again the polished plates of rust, familiar handholds of survival. This battered piece of tubing was his first tool—and weapon, he reflected, thinking of Proctor. The tramp had not yet put in an appearance, but Maitland scanned the grass and nettle banks, certain that he was lurking somewhere in the undergrowth.

His confidence returning, Maitland climbed down from the roof of the outhouse. He steadied himself on the crutch, standing upright again. His trousers hung in rags from the waistband, but he felt strong and determined. When he pressed his skull he could feel barbs of pain at the loosened sutures. The concussion and fever had cleared, leaving him with no more than a light continuous headache.

Maitland looked up at the motorway embankments. He knew that he was probably strong enough to climb the earth slopes, but Proctor would be watching him, waiting for Maitland to make a move. Another physical confrontation with the tramp would set him back several days. Somehow he must get the girl to help him. She alone had any authority over Proctor.

Maitland swung himself back to the ruined cinema. Pressing through the grass, he reached the stairwell and lowered his injured leg down the steps to the basement room.

He sat on the bed in the half-light, breaking the rusks in his hands. The child's food cut his mouth, and he chewed carefully on the sharp spurs of sweet toast. He reached out with the crutch and pulled the girl's suitcase towards him. He searched through the dresses and underwear, thinking that she might, conceivably, own some small weapon.

At the bottom of the case, in the debris of make-up tubes, hairpins and used tissues, was a packet of fading snapshots. Curious about her background, Maitland spread the photographs out on the bed. One showed a strong-faced adolescent girl, clearly Jane, standing protectively beside a faded middle-aged woman with glazed eyes on the frayed lawn of a small sanatorium. In another she was visiting a fairground, arm-in-arm with a heavyset man twenty years older than herself. Maitland assumed that the man was her father, but a wedding photograph showed Jane, proudly six months pregnant, standing in a church beside the man, the fey-looking mother hovering in the background like a deranged ghost.

A second man appeared in the series, a dapper figure of about fifty in an old but well-made suit, posed beside a white Bentley in the drive of a large Victorian house. Her father, Maitland decided, or perhaps another middle-aged lover. What had happened to the child?

Maitland gathered the photographs together and put them back into the case. From an empty tissue box he took out a brown paper bag. Inside it were the materials of a pot-smoker's kit—scraps of burnt silver foil, detached filter stubs, loose tobacco from broken cigarettes, a small block of hashish, cigarette papers and a roller, and a box of matches.

Replacing the paper bag, Maitland weighed the matchbox in his hand. His eyes moved swiftly around the room. From the packing case he pulled out the paraffin stove. He swirled the contents in the half-light, listening to the soft liquid sound.

Ten minutes later, Maitland hobbled on the crutch towards the ruined outhouse. The red blanket was draped over one shoulder, and in his free hand he carried the paraffin stove. He pulled himself on to the roof and sat down on the shallow tiled slope, arranging the stove and blanket beside him. After making certain that neither Proctor nor the young woman was approaching, he tied a corner of the blanket to the crutch, and soaked the loose end of the woollen fabric in the paraffin from the stove.

Along the motorway the flow of Sunday afternoon traffic was intermittent. Maitland watched, matchbox in hand, controlling his eagerness. A line of saloon cars appeared, hemmed in behind an airline coach and a fuel tanker moving abreast through the overpass tunnel.

Maitland struck two of the matches and lit the blanket. The warm paraffin ignited with a soft purr, the low flames caressing the worn fabric. Black smoke lifted into the air. Maitland stood up, balancing on one leg, and began to semaphore with the burning blanket. He choked on a billow of acrid smoke and sat down, lifted himself up again and waved the blanket to and fro.

As he expected, Proctor and the young woman soon appeared on the scene. The tramp moved through the grass in a low crouch, like some wary beast, his scarred hands parting the blades. His crafty but stupid eyes were fixed on Maitland as if he were a trapper's quarry ready to be staked and skinned. By contrast, Jane Sheppard strolled sedately along the uneven ground, as if she had no interest in Maitland's attempt to escape.

'I thought you two would turn up!' Maitland shouted. 'Right, Proctor?'

He climbed down from the roof of the outhouse and waved the burning blanket in Proctor's face, making the tramp grunt and curse. Maitland lunged forward at him, choking on the smoke, dropped to one knee and picked up the paraffin stove. As Proctor snatched at the blanket, tearing away a ragged square of burning wool, Maitland dashed the stove on to the ground and swung the blanket through the spilt liquid.

Moving on all fours, Proctor circled Maitland cautiously. The young woman reached the outhouse, dividing the grass with her small hands. Waving away the smoke in her face, she shouted at Proctor:

'Put it out! Never mind him! They'll see the smoke!'

The charred blanket fell from the end of the crutch. Maitland scooped up the bundle of smoking rags, but Proctor lunged forward and snatched the blanket away. He stamped out the flames, kicking the loose soil over the smouldering fibres.

Maitland leaned weakly on the crutch. He waved at the passing cars, but no one had stopped or even noticed this brief episode. He turned to face Proctor. The tramp picked up a worn half-brick and circled Maitland like a boxer. Maitland darted forward, striking Proctor on the shoulder with the crutch. His rising blood pressure pumped against the loose sutures of his skull, but landing this single blow exhilarated him. His left foot slipped on the broken flagstones around the outhouse. He caught his balance and whirled the crutch through the air.

Crouching down, shoulders below his hips, Proctor evaded the swinging crutch with a ducking movement of his bull-necked head. His white face, like a dried pumpkin, was without expression as his eyes measured Maitland's long legs and arms.

'Stop it . . . !'

Holding her red hair to the nape of her neck like a bored housewife settling a street fracas, Jane Sheppard stepped up to Maitland. She seized the metal pipe, trying to lower it to the ground. 'For heaven's sake . . .' She gazed at Maitland with her severe child's eyes. 'Aren't you carrying things a little too far?'

Maitland glanced at the scanty traffic behind him. Proctor was squatting beside a bank of nettles, the half-brick waiting in his hand. They would not risk killing him here in the open. Three derelicts burning an old blanket would attract no attention, but a brutal fight might arouse the interest of an off-duty policeman.

'Proctor,' Maitland said, pointing the crutch at Jane. 'She has the keys, you know. The keys to my car.'

'What?' The young woman glared at Maitland, genuinely outraged. 'What keys are you talking about?'

'Proctor . . .' The tramp was watching. 'The keys to the trunk of my car. My wallet was in there.'

'That's nonsense.' The young woman turned to leave. 'Come on, let's go.'

'You couldn't unlock the trunk, could you, Proctor?' Maitland hobbled forward, the metal crutch held out like a lance. Proctor's eyes were moving between the girl and Maitland. 'There was thirty pounds in my wallet.'

'Proctor, ignore him! He's insane, he'll call the police.' Confused and angry, she picked up a large brick and offered it to Proctor.

'The two of you searched me last night, Proctor,' Maitland said quietly. He was only six feet away from the tramp, well within range of a bull-like rush. 'You know damn well I haven't been back to the car—you keep an eye on me all the time.'

As Jane waited impatiently for Proctor to strike him, Maitland took the wallet from his pocket. He spread the pound notes in a greasy fan in front of Proctor's face. 'Who gave it to me, Proctor? Who took it from the car? Here, take one . . .'

The tramp stared mesmerized at the pound notes. He turned to look at Jane, standing with more stones in her hands, her face a mask of confused hostility.

'No one's ever given you anything before, have they, Proctor?' Maitland said. 'Go on, take it.'

As the tramp's scarred hand closed shyly over the damp banknote
Maitland leaned exhausted against the crutch.

Wary of each other, the three of them made their way back to the
cinema. The young woman took Maitland's arm and helped him
through the grass, muttering angrily to herself. Proctor followed
them, carrying the tattered blanket and the paraffin stove. His
creased face was without expression. As Maitland climbed down
the staircase he saw that Proctor was crouching like a nervous animal, unsure whether to assert his dominion over the island.

14

a taste of poison

'What the hell were you playing at?' The young woman steered
Maitland on to the bed with a hard hand. Her strong body was
livid with temper. 'You're supposed to be a sick man! I'm not inter-
ested in fighting over a wallet. I've a damned good mind to pack up
and leave you here before you cause any more trouble.'

'He tried to kill me,' Maitland said. 'You were egging him on.'

'I wasn't. Anyway, Proctor's half blind. That was our blanket you
set fire to.'

'Your blanket. I'm not staying here tonight.'

'Nobody wants you to.' The girl shook her head with unfeigned
indignation. 'That's real capitalist gratitude! I saved you from Proctor just now, and you tell him about the wallet. That was pretty
smart of you, giving him money. It won't do you any good—Proctor
never leaves this place and as far as I know there's nowhere here to
spend it.'

Maitland shook his head. 'It wasn't smart at all. Poor old man,
I don't think he knew how to take it.'

'The only thing he's been given is other people's shit. Don't get any ideas about him being your friend for life. If I left you alone with him you'd soon miss me.'

Maitland watched her pacing about restlessly. Her repeated references to leaving the island worried him. He was not yet ready to deal with Proctor on his own.

'Jane—sooner or later, you'll have to help me. My friends and family, the police, my office, they're bound to find out what happened here. They must be looking for me now.'

'*Your* family . . .' The girl had taken this isolated phrase from its context, putting a peculiar emphasis on it. 'What about my family?' She swung away and snapped, 'I haven't taken a penny from you— tell them that!'

Tired and cold, Maitland lay back against the damp pillow. The young woman moved around the dimly lit room. She straightened her suitcase, and re-hung her clothes. The afternoon light was fading, and Maitland regretted that he had burned the blanket. He realized that he had gained a small advantage over the girl and Proctor. Already he was playing these two outcasts against each other, feeding their mutual distrust.

Yet for the time being he was the young woman's prisoner, and a prey to whatever devious whims might flick through her mind. In an odd way she seemed to enjoy their relationship. Her attitude towards him varied from tenderness and good humour to a sudden vengeful anger, almost as if he represented two different people for her. After hanging her clothes she lit the stove and made Maitland a drink of condensed milk and hot water. She held his head in her arm, crooning reassuringly as he drank from the plastic cup, half-working her plump breast against his forehead as if feeding her own baby. A minute later, in an abrupt change of mood, she pulled herself away sharply, jarring Maitland's head. She began to prowl irritably around the room, and turned up the paraffin lamp in a complaining way as if blaming Maitland for the falling afternoon light.

'Jane . . .' Maitland pulled out his oil-stained wallet. 'Do you want this money? You could use it to get away from here.' He held out the wallet, feeling a sudden surge of concern for the girl.

'I don't want to get away from here. Why should I?' She turned her head with a flourish, watching him suspiciously.

'Jane, be serious. You can't stay in this place for ever—where's your family? You were married, weren't you?' Maitland pointed to the suitcase, adding frankly, 'I looked through your photographs. Your husband—what happened?'

'Mind—your—own—damn—business.' She spoke in firm, quiet tones. Her fingers stiffened like rods. 'God Almighty, I came here to get away from all these moral attitudes.' She blundered around the room, as if searching for an exit from Maitland's nagging. 'People are never happier than when they're inventing new vices.'

'Jane, say I promised you five hundred pounds—would you help me to leave?'

She glanced at him cannily. 'Why so much? That's a lot of money.'

'Because I want us both to get away from here. I think we need each other's help. I'll give you five hundred pounds—I'm serious.'

'Five hundred pounds . . .' She appeared to consider his offer, mentally counting each one of a stack of bills. Abruptly she turned on him, gesturing with her pot smoker's brown paper bag. 'Have you any idea how long that would rent a house for a homeless family?'

'Jane—you're part of a homeless family. Your child–'

Maitland gave up. He lay back wearily as Jane spread out her kit. For a minute she sat slackly on the edge of the bed, ignoring Maitland's hand which he placed reassuringly on her arm. Her eyes stared at the shabby wall. Mechanically, she prepared two cigarettes, and wrapped away the kit in its paper bag. Rattling the matchbox as if to revive herself, she lit the first of the cigarettes. She inhaled deeply on the sweet smoke, holding it in her lungs for several seconds. Satisfied, she lay down next to Maitland, nudging him to move over. She pulled her combat jacket over them, smiling wanly to herself as she gazed at the Astaire and Rogers poster.

Maitland felt his mind swaying under the effects of the smoke. The young woman's strong body pressed against his own as the bed sank in its centre. Her arm rose and fell. She lifted the cigarette to her lips, and offered him a draw. Trying to keep himself alert, and frightened of falling asleep, Maitland fixed his eyes on the fading light coming down the stair well. His fever was returning with the cold evening air.

The young woman smiled at him, taking his hand lightly. Her strong-jawed face lay like a child's in its bower of red hair. She released the smoke from her mouth and steered it towards him with her hand.

'Nice . . . ? You know, you could have got away from here, if you'd wanted to.'

'How?'

'Right at the beginning . . .' She inhaled on the cigarette. 'If you'd really tried, you could have done.'

'Tried?' With a grimace Maitland recalled his ordeal in the rain.

He rubbed his chest, covered by no more than the grimy dress shirt. 'It's cold in here.'

The young woman stretched her arm across him. 'You could have got away,' she repeated. 'Proctor doesn't realize this, but you made it easy for him. Do you know that we both thought you might have been here before?'

She gazed through the smoke at Maitland, and stroked the oil-smeared ruff of his shirt. He watched her without speaking. Her tone was in no way jeering or hostile, but at the same time she seemed to be testing both him and herself, exploring through Maitland some failure in her own past. With an unerring eye for the defects of others, she had seen that he would accept this role.

Had he, in fact, deliberately marooned himself on the island? He remembered his refusal to walk through the overpass tunnel to the emergency telephone, his childish insistence that a rush-hour driver stop for him, the anger that had poured out . . . he had sat in that empty bath as a child, screaming with the same resentment.

Deciding to play the girl's game, he said, 'Jane, you owe it to yourself to leave here—by staying on the island you're just punishing yourself.'

'Big deal—I don't get that.' Her eyes glinted in her cold, euphoric face. 'Anyway, it's easier than coming to terms with something. I was never very good at patching up quarrels—I wanted to go on simmering for days. That way you can really hate . . .'

She smoked the last of the cigarette. When she had finished it she placed her hand on Maitland's stomach. Moving her head, she kissed him on the mouth.

'Don't tell me I touched a nerve?' she asked.

'Perhaps you did.' Maitland tried to put his arm around her waist, but his fever was rolling in waves across his body. 'These last four days have been strange—like visiting an insane asylum and seeing yourself sitting on a bench.'

He slipped away from her. Vaguely he was aware of her undressing. As she smoked the second cigarette she examined her stomach and breasts in the travelling mirror. She changed into a short, blood-red skirt and sleeveless lurex blouse. He had already fallen asleep when she turned down the lamp and left the room, her stiletto heels clattering on the stairs.

Hours later, in the centre of the night, he heard her return. The traffic sounds had gone, and as she argued with Proctor her sharp voice carried clearly over the seething grass. The tramp seemed to be remonstrating with her, whining that she had forgotten to bring something for him. When she came into the room she turned up the lamp and glared down drunkenly at Maitland. Her wild hair flamed around her in the vivid light like a demented sun.

She clattered among the cans and saucepans, barely able to focus her eyes. Maitland watched her uneasily. Her behaviour warned him that she might be mentally disturbed, perhaps a fugitive from a Broadmoor institution. Was it Jane, and not her mother, who had been the inmate of the sanatorium in the photograph? Too weak to protect himself, he listened to the cosmetics tumbling from the card table. A poster ripped in her hands as she swayed around the room, tearing Manson's face. When she brought a cup over to him and held his head he drank gratefully in his fever.

Gasping for breath, he choked on the dilute paraffin she had fed him. He vomited into her hands and lay retching across the bed. He tried to hold off the girl as she tottered towards him with a glass of milk, laughing into his face.

Behind her, Proctor burst into the room. The polished lapels of his dinner jacket gleamed like mirrors in the blazing light. Pushing Jane aside, he bent over Maitland and wiped the paraffin from his face. She screamed at him, flinging the vomit-smeared combat jacket after them as Proctor carried Maitland up the staircase and laid him on the wet midnight grass.

15

the bribe

The morning traffic, opening the new week, moved along the eastbound lanes of the motorway. Robert Maitland sat against the curved roof of the air-raid shelter in which Proctor had made his home, watching the sharp sunlight cut across the polished cellulose of the vehicles driving into central London. It was shortly after eight o'clock, and the cool air refreshed him after the night of fever. His injured leg lay in front of him. The hip joint was still stiff, needing some kind of surgical intervention, but the deep abrasions on the thigh had begun to heal.

In spite of his inability to walk, Maitland felt calm and determined. The last traces of his fever had receded. His stomach was filled with the crude meal Proctor had prepared for him—sweet tea and a surprisingly appetising gruel of cold fried potatoes, pieces of fatty meat and coleslaw which Maitland had devoured. The taste of paraffin still filled his mouth and lungs, but he inhaled the fresh scents of the grass forest that grew around his legs.

He watched Proctor cleaning out the shelter. This deep burrow, where Maitland had spent the night, was little more than a large kennel, its walls lined with patched quilts. After being carried there on the tramp's powerful back, Maitland had lain half-conscious on a mattress by the doorway, while Proctor moved about his den like a hard-working and insecure animal. Everything in the shelter was locked away in a series of wooden boxes below the quilts and mattresses. During the night, whenever Maitland began to retch emptily, trying to vomit away the paraffin that filled his lungs, Proctor agitated himself in a nervous hunt. He lifted up corners of the quilts and replaced them as he searched for a forgotten cubbyhole. Eventually he produced a shallow pail and a roll of cotton waste. For an hour he sat beside Maitland, wiping his eyes and mouth. In the light reflected from the evening motorway his broad face with its universe of creases hovered above Maitland like an anxious beast's. All night he moved restlessly around his burrow, keeping up a continuous pointless activity. The quilted floor merged into the walls, as if the lair had been designed to blunt and muffle all evidence of the world outside.

Maitland watched the traffic move past along the motorway. The embankments seemed further away than he remembered them, slowly receding from him on all sides. By contrast the island appeared far larger, covered by a dense and luxuriant growth. Maitland shivered in the cool morning air. Through the doorway of the shelter he could see his dinner jacket hanging beside the threadbare leotard.

Proctor's head emerged from the den. He scrutinized Maitland for several seconds before the rest of his body came into view.

Maitland clasped his shoulders. 'Proctor—I'm cold. Have you got a coat? I won't ask you for my dinner jacket.'

'Aah . . . no coat.' Proctor said regretfully. He began to rub Maitland's arms in his strong hands. Patiently, Maitland pushed him away.

'Look—I need something to wear. You don't want me to catch fever again–?'

'No more fever . . .' Proctor glanced at Maitland's watch on his wrist as if its luminous dial might solve this problem. He pulled out the winder and rotated the hands at random. Satisfied, he showed the watch to Maitland. The new time-setting seemed to make him more comfortable. 'No more fever for Mr Maitland,' he announced, but a moment later he bounded down into the shelter and rooted under his quilts. He returned with an old woollen shawl.

Maitland draped the yellowing garment around his heavy shoulders, ignoring the sweet, musty smell. Proctor hovered from one foot to the next, almost as if he were awaiting instructions. Despite his sudden moods of violence, the tramp was a placid and warm-hearted man, with the natural dignity of a large, simple animal.

Proctor kicked away the loose stones lying in the grass outside the shelter and began to practise his gymnastics, clearly with the intention of impressing Maitland. After a clumsy forward somersault he attempted a crude cartwheel, and landed on his head in a heap. Sitting there, he examined his hands and feet, as if mystified why they should fail him.

'Proctor . . .' Maitland chose his words carefully. 'I'm going to leave here today. I must go home—do you understand? You've got your home here, and I've got mine. I have a wife and a son—they need me. Now, I'm grateful to you for looking after me . . .'

He stopped, realizing that the last sentence was the only one which had registered on the tramp's mind.

'Listen to me, Proctor—I want you to help me climb the embankment. Now!'

He held out his arm to Proctor, but the tramp glanced uneasily towards the ruined cinema. 'Help Mr Maitland . . . how? Maitland's sick.'

Doggedly, Maitland controlled his anger. 'Proctor, you're strong enough to carry me. Help me and I won't tell the police you're here. If you keep me here any longer they'll take you away—put you into an institution. You don't want to spend the rest of your life in prison?'

'No!' Proctor shouted the word vehemently. He looked around carefully, as if nervous that a passing driver might have heard him. 'No prison for Proctor.'

'No,' Maitland agreed. Even this brief conversation was exhausting him. 'I don't want to send you to prison. After all, you've helped me, Proctor.'

'Yes . . .' Proctor nodded vigorously. 'Proctor *helped* Mr Maitland.'

'Right, then.' Maitland hoisted himself on to the crutch and swayed unsteadily as the blood left his head. He tried to hold Proctor's shoulder, but the tramp stepped back. Maitland pointed himself in the direction of the motorway embankment. The westbound lane was almost deserted, but on the far side of the central reservation the three lanes of traffic pressed towards central London.

'Proctor! Over here—give me a hand!'

The tramp stood his ground, slowly shaking his huge creased head. 'No . . .' he said finally, staring at Maitland's gaunt and ragged figure as if no longer recognizing it. 'Miss Jane . . .'

Before Maitland could protest he had turned and scuttled into the long grass, head bent below the waving blades.

Reviving himself on the cold air, Maitland wrapped the shawl tightly around his chest and set off alone towards the embankment.

Proctor's refusal to help him, and the tramp's evident fear of the young woman, did not surprise him. They were part of that conspiracy of the grotesque which had kept him marooned on the island, for what was now his fifth day. He thrashed at the grass in front of him, identifying its luxuriant growth with all the pain he had felt.

Even this short journey across the island exhausted him. After the meagre breakfast of scraps he was already ravenous again. Each day that passed had fractionally cut away his strength. The deep grass jostled around him on all sides like a hostile crowd. Swaying unsteadily, Maitland pressed on across the central valley. By the time he reached the breaker's yard with its semicircle of rusty vehicles he was almost too tired to identify the crashed Jaguar.

The sky had clouded over, and a cold drizzle fell through the retreating sunlight. Maitland climbed into the rear seat of the car, his home for his first days on the island. As he tried to massage a little warmth into his stick-like arms he thought hard about Proctor and Jane Sheppard. Somehow he must devise a means of dominating them. At any moment they might simply lose interest in him altogether, leaving him to perish inside the hull of this burnt-out car. Maitland looked up at the embankment—not only had the slope become steeper than he remembered it, but the hard shoulder and balustrade seemed twenty feet higher.

First, he needed a bribe. Climbing from the car, he took out his keys. He opened the trunk. Inside the carton were the last three bottles of white Burgundy. He secured one of the bottles inside the shawl, locked the trunk and set off for Proctor's den.

The doorway to the shelter was padlocked. Catching his breath after the effect of re-crossing the island, Maitland leaned on the crutch in the thin rain. The tramp was squatting by the gutter of the feeder road embankment, patiently filling a tin bucket with water dripping from the face of the route indicator seventy feet above him.

He returned to the shelter when he saw Maitland, moving like a large mole through the grass. Two mess-tins rattled from his waist-belt. In his right hand he held a clutch of some half-dozen spring traps. A pair of small rats hung from the trap-jaws, their long tails swinging together. Looking at him, Maitland remembered the injured rat who had climbed across his leg. Presumably Proctor supplemented his meagre diet with these field rodents. Yet somewhere he had access to other food sources. Once he could discover these, Maitland's tenancy of the island would be more secure.

'Proctor—I need food. I'll pass out soon if I don't get something to eat.'

The tramp stared at him warily. He raised the rattraps, but Maitland shook his head.

'No food,' Proctor said flatly.

'That's rubbish—we had breakfast. Meat, potatoes, salad—where did you get it?'

Proctor's eyes were drifting away, as if he were about to lose interest in the discussion. Maitland pulled the bottle of wine from his shawl. 'Wine, Proctor—wine for food. Let's exchange.'

He held out the bottle to the tramp, who raised the cork to his nose, sniffing at the metal foil.

'All right—Proctor take you to the food place.'

16

the food source

They set off along the central valley towards the overpass. Maitland swung himself clumsily on the metal crutch, wishing that he could disconnect his right leg and throw it away. Proctor scurried ahead, his body bent horizontally at the waist, always below the level of the grass canopy. He deliberately sought out the areas of deepest growth, as if he were most at home in the invisible corridors that he had tunnelled in his endless passages around the island.

They approached the wire-mesh fence below the overpass. As they emerged from the grass, like swimmers coming ashore, Proctor gazed uncertainly at the concrete parapets around them. The magnified roar of the traffic unsettled him, and he seemed almost bemused now that he had left the sanctuary of the island and its green swaying ocean. Maitland noticed that the tramp moved his head as if he could barely focus on any distant object and, like a bird, relied on being able to react to brief sharp movements against the background of a static visual field. Watching him, Maitland visualized the half-blind acrobat, irises occluded

by gathering cataracts, no longer able to see the surrounding traffic streams and living alone in this forgotten world whose furthest
shores were defined only by the roar of automobile engines, the
humming of tyres and squeal of brake linings. For Proctor, as
Maitland had seen already, the deep grass was his vital medium.
His scarred hands felt the flexing stems, reading their currents
as they seethed around him. He thought of Proctor emerging
from his den in the seconds after the crash, feeling the impact
of the Jaguar jarring through the grass in a series of warning
ripples . . .

Proctor nudged his arm. Darting into the oily shadows below
the overpass, he scuttled towards the southern end of the wire-mesh
fence. He climbed the shallow slope of the embankment and lay on
his stomach, his face pressed against the fence. He turned and beckoned to Maitland, pulling him up the slope.

Lying beside the tramp, Maitland watched him force his scarred
fingers through the steel mesh. In the dim light Maitland could see
an amorphous mass of gleaming mucilage which lay in a three-feet-
high heap across a stack of truck tyres. The nearest edge of this
sludge pile was already oozing through the mesh. Pressing his fingers through the fence, Proctor picked at the slices of wet bread,
lumps of fatty meat and vegetable scraps embedded in the greasy
avalanche.

This illicit garbage dump, Maitland assumed, was used by a local restaurant or food mart. Proctor unclipped the mess-tins from
his belt. He showed their polished interiors to Maitland, indicating how clean they were. Already he had reclaimed two slices of wet
bread and a nub of beef gristle. Although forbidding himself to eat
now, he licked his fingers appreciatively. He urged Maitland forward, sliding a mess tin across to him.

Maitland stared at the fragments in Proctor's tin. He knew now where Proctor had found their meal that morning. Yet he felt no sense of revulsion, but only a flat pity for the tramp. Despite his own injuries, the insult to Proctor's body seemed far greater.

Trying to devise some means of rescuing both the tramp and himself, he waited for Proctor as the macerated food gleamed in the tacky light below the overpass.

When they returned to Proctor's den the rain had ended. Maitland sat against the shelter, watching the passing traffic. The rush hour had ended, but a steady stream of cars and buses moved through the sunlight.

Proctor squatted down happily to this early lunch, eyeing the scraps of food in both mess-tins. After an elaborate pause he made his decision, handing Maitland the larger portion. With his clasp knife he cut the cork from the wine bottle and sat next to Maitland, beckoning him to eat. Despite this generosity, he obviously has no intention of sharing the wine with Maitland.

'Mr Maitland, eat,' Proctor said firmly, already tucking into the scraps with a strong appetite. 'It's good food today, good for Maitland's leg.'

He lifted the wine bottle to his lips.

Within ten minutes Proctor was drunk. Although he had swallowed little more than a third of the bottle, even this small quantity of alcohol had bolted through his brain, kicking away its fragile supports. He rolled from side to side, gabbling happily to himself and twisting his face into grotesque expressions. He slid

over to Maitland when he saw the untouched food and gesticu-
lated blearily.

'Do you want this, Proctor?' Maitland asked. 'I bet it was tasty.'

The tramp rolled about, dribbling the wine from his mouth. He
went through a pantomime of reassuring Maitland that he would
never take his food, but a moment later he had seized the mess-tin
and was cramming the soggy fragments into his mouth. He touched
Maitland on the arm and shoulder at various points, as if identifying him in his clouding mind. He sat close to Maitland, clearly glad
to have him as a friend.

'It's good here on the island, isn't it, Proctor?' Maitland said. He
felt a surge of affection for the tramp.

'It's good . . .' Proctor nodded muzzily. Most of the wine was
running down the furrows of his cheeks and chin. He put an arm
around Maitland's shoulders, testing this new friend.

'When are you going to leave here, Proctor?'

'Aah . . . never leave here.' Proctor lifted the bottle to his mouth,
then lowered it and gazed sadly at the ground. 'There's nowhere for
Proctor to go.'

'I suppose that's true.' Maitland watched Proctor stroke his
arm. 'Isn't there anyone who could look after you—any family or
friends?'

Proctor stared blankly into the air, as if trying to fathom this
question. He leaned across Maitland, seizing his shoulders like a
drunk in a bar, and said with crafty humour, 'Mr Maitland is Proctor's friend.'

'Right. I'm your friend. I have to be, don't I?' As the tramp pawed
at his arm, Maitland felt the full extent of his insecurity, the fear
that his last hiding place, appropriately in the centre of this alien-
ating city, would be taken from him. At the same time, Maitland

guessed that the tramp's mind was beginning to fade, and that he dimly perceived that he needed help and friendship.

'Proctor needs a . . . friend.' He coughed out a spray of wine.

'I guess you do.' Maitland clambered to his feet. He disengaged his left leg from Proctor's embrace. Proctor rolled back against the shelter, smiling to himself over the bottle of wine.

Maitland hobbled away, crossing the central valley to the higher ground on the northern side of the island. The sight of the traffic dulled his hunger. He felt faint and unsteady, but his nerves were calm. He surveyed the green triangle which had been his home for the past five days. Its dips and hollows, rises and hillocks he knew as intimately as his own body. Moving across it, he seemed to be following a contour line inside his head.

The grass was quiet, barely moving around him. Standing there, like a shepherd with a silent flock, he thought of the strange phrase he had muttered to himself during his delirium: I am the island.

Ten minutes later, as he reached the breaker's yard, an orange Toyota estate car emerged from the tunnel of the overpass. It cruised along the west-bound carriageway, its bright bodywork gleaming in the sunlight. Through the balustrade Maitland saw the face of the driver, a blonde-haired woman with a high-bridged nose and firm mouth. Her small but strong hands were held together at the top of the steering wheel in a characteristic pose.

'Catherine . . . ! Stop . . . !' Maitland shouted into the air. The car, unmistakably his wife's, slowed as it approached the rear of an airline bus. Unsure whether he was seeing an hallucination brought on by his hunger, Maitland swung himself rapidly through the grass. He stopped to wave the crutch, stumbled and fell to the ground. By the time he picked himself up, shouting angrily at the grass, the car had accelerated away.

Maitland turned his back to the motorway. Almost certainly, Catherine had been visiting the office, presumably to discuss his disappearance with his two partners. This meant that none of them realized he had crashed on to a small patch of waste ground literally within view of their windows.

Gripping the metal crutch, Maitland swung himself towards the air-raid shelter. Somehow, before his strength gave out, he would force himself up the embankment.

Fifty feet from the shelter, he heard Jane Sheppard call out, 'Go on, Proctor—now! It's none of his business. Put it on before he comes.'

17

the duel

As Maitland approached the air-raid shelter Proctor and the young woman were cavorting about in the open air by the entrance. Proctor tottered to and fro, the half-empty wine bottle still clasped in his thick hand. His feet stumbled in and out of the lid of Maitland's overnight case—Jane had evidently removed it from the car when she searched for his wallet.

Proctor lurched away from Maitland as the tall man swung himself forward on the crutch. He had taken off his patchwork denims and forced his legs into Maitland's evening-dress trousers. The sweet scent of hash hung in the air. Smoke drifted from the leaking stub in Jane's mouth as she knelt at Proctor's feet, trying to turn up the trousers.

Proctor pushed back the sleeves of the dinner jacket, fastening around his wrists the pair of cuffs which Jane had torn from the spare dress shirt. The collar and a ragged bib of flowered shirt were already around his neck. Maitland's black tie jutted at a rakish

angle under one ear as he wiped the wine from his mouth, simpering
happily to himself.

'Right! You look a treat!' Jane stepped back to survey her handi-
work, enjoying this drunken parody of a wine waiter. She turned a
funless smile towards Maitland, swaying up to him.

'Don't look so serious, Mr Maitland. Come and join us—we're
having a party.'

'So I see. Who's the guest of honour?'

Maitland swung himself forward, striking Proctor's unsteady
feet with the metal crutch. Proctor staggered back, grinning ami-
ably over his bottle. His puckered face, every crease lit by its veins,
was a clown's mask. He looked up at Maitland with an expression
of pride and obsequiousness, hostility confused in his clouding
mind with a keen need to earn Maitland's approval. He raised the
bottle in a toast, and leaned blearily against the curved wall of the
shelter, his overblown belly bursting the top button of the trousers. As he clutched at them delightedly, Jane danced around
him, snapping her fingers. She was still wearing the tart's outfit
of the previous night, and her high stiletto heels caught in the
stony ground.

'Come on!' she shouted to Maitland. 'Stop looking so long-faced.
You can't enjoy yourself!' She slapped Proctor's head, only half-
playfully. 'God, look at you both!'

Maitland waited calmly as they played the fool with him, the
girl urging Proctor to pour the wine over him. Proctor staggered
about in the burst dinner jacket, black tie at the back of his neck,
cuffs falling off his wrists.

'Come on, you're going to dance for me!' Jane shouted into
Maitland's face. 'Do a one-legged dance! Proctor, make him dance
for me!'

Proctor blundered into Maitland, eyes no longer synchronized. Jane bent down and rooted around in the overnight case.

'There's a letter here—from a woman doctor. Not a very professional relationship, I must say. Listen to this, Proctor . . .'

Maitland stepped forward, pushing Proctor away. The tramp's acid breath gusted into his face. Proctor fell back against the shelter in a spray of wine. He sat helplessly on the ground. As Jane started to upend the case, Maitland lifted the crutch and drove it into the open lid, striking it from her hands. Startled, she crouched away angrily.

'What the hell are you—'

'Right!' Matter-of-factly, Maitland lifted the crutch and beckoned her from the case. She edged back along the ground, pointing to the recumbent Proctor.

'Wait till he wakes . . . Believe me, he'll—'

'He'll do nothing. Take my word for it.'

Maitland stepped towards Proctor. The tramp gazed up at him, embarrassed by his own drunkenness. He tried to straighten the bow tie under his ear, smiling apologetically at Maitland. He waited without expression when Maitland stood over him, unfastening his trouser vent.

As the urine struck his face, Proctor raised his scarred hands. He stared at the amber liquid splashing on to his palms and pouring down the lapels of his dinner jacket. Unable to move his body, he looked passively at Maitland. The jet of urine hit the tramp's mouth and eyes, frothing on his shoulders. The hot drops bubbled and seethed in the dust around him.

Maitland waited until he had finished. Proctor lay stranded on his side in the pool of urine, his eyes lowered. With one hand he tried to clean the dinner jacket, brushing sadly at the lapels.

Ignoring Proctor now, Maitland turned towards the young woman. She had watched the episode without moving. He pointed to the scattered contents of the overnight case.

'All right, Jane? Now, gather everything up.'

Without hesitating, she knelt down by the case. Quickly she replaced the dress shoes and towel. Sober now, she stared calmly at Maitland.

'He won't forget that.'

'He wasn't intended to.' As she locked the case Maitland beckoned her towards the cinema. 'We'll go back to your room.'

When Jane stood her ground, sharp eyes searching Maitland's bearded face for any signs of fever, Maitland reached out and tried to cuff her across the head. She stepped back nimbly.

'I won't help you to get away from here.'

'Never mind. As a matter of fact, I don't particularly want to get away from here. Not for the moment, anyway.'

Without looking back at Proctor, lying passively in the pool of urine, he swung himself after the young woman. She walked in front of him, head down, carrying the overnight case.

18

five pounds

'Where's the lamp? Let's have some light in this little hell.'

Maitland pulled himself through the doorway of the darkened basement room, almost crushing Jane's shoulders. He sat on the dishevelled bed, his injured leg stretched out like a tattered pole. Holding the crutch in his right hand, he tapped the floor.

'Light the stove as well. I want some hot water. You're going to wash me.'

Glancing warily at Maitland, Jane put herself to work. She filled a saucepan with water from the fifty-gallon drum in the stair well, pumped up the paraffin stove and lit the flame.

'That was a bastard thing to do to that old fool.'

'It was meant to be,' Maitland said. 'I've no intention of being played around with by a senile tramp and a neurotic runaway.'

'It was still a bastard thing to do. You must be a real shit.'

Maitland let this pass. His new-found aggressive role, although completely calculated, had subdued the young woman. He pulled off his shirt. His arms and chest were covered with grease and bruise marks.

'You ought to clean out this room,' he told the girl. 'Did you have your miscarriage here?'

'It was nothing to do with this room!' Bridling, she stood up. With an effort, she checked her anger. 'Are you trying to play on my sense of guilt? I take it that's your grand strategy now?'

'I'm glad it's that obvious.'

'Well, don't. I feel bad enough without you turning your two-edged sword in the wound.'

Maitland kicked the packing case, rattling the pans inside it. 'I need some food—let's see what you've got. And none of that infant feed you keep bringing for me. I'm not going to play the part of your baby.'

Stung, the girl retorted, 'I suppose you think that's why I've kept you here.'

'I wouldn't be surprised. I'm not deriding your little maudlin outbursts, they'd be very sweet in the right place, but I've got other things on my mind. One, two and three, I want out.'

Jane rolled up the grimy dress shirt. 'I'll wash this for you. Listen, I'll call for help—when I'm ready. You keep thinking of yourself all the time. Can't you understand that I may have problems of my own?'

'With the police?'

'Yes! With the police!' Furiously, she pulled a metal pail from beneath the bed and poured the hot water into it.

'What was it?' Maitland asked. 'Drugs, abortion—or are you on the run from a remand home?'

Jane paused, her hands motionless in the water.

'Clever,' she commented quietly. 'You must do very well in your business, Mr Maitland—but not so well in your private life, I'd guess.' She added, in a limp voice, 'I borrowed some money. From a friend of my husband. Rather a lot of money, in fact. Lousy bastard.'

She began to wash Maitland, her hands soaping his bruised skin. When she had finished she found a cosmetic razor and shaved his beard. Maitland sat on the edge of the bed, enjoying the gentle pressure of her small hands moving across his skin like submissive birds. He was surprised that it had pleased him, even slightly, to humiliate the young woman, playing on her muddled feelings of guilt and deriding her in a way that he had never thought himself capable of doing. By contrast, his humiliation of Proctor had been entirely calculated; he had degraded the old tramp in the crudest way he could. But even this brutal act had given him a certain pleasure. He had relished the violent confrontation, knowing that he would make both of them submit to him. In part, he was taking his revenge on Proctor and the young woman, although he was well aware that both of them, by some paradoxical logic, were satisfied by being abused. Maitland's aggressiveness fulfilled their expectations, their half-conscious estimates of themselves. Much as he distrusted himself for enjoying these small cruelties, Maitland had deliberately egged himself on. Determined to survive above all else, he would exploit this strain of cruelty in himself in the same way that he had earlier exploited his self-pity and contempt. All that mattered was that he dominate the senile tramp and this wayward young woman.

He let the girl towel him down. Her hands, steering between the bruises, calmed and soothed him.

'What about your father?' he asked her. 'Could he help you?'

'He's not my father any more. I don't think about him.' She

gazed at the sunlight coming down the stair well, clasping her hands in what seemed to be a Masonic grip. 'Suicide is . . . a suggestive act, it runs in families, you know. When someone in your family reaches the point where they cannot just kill themselves, but take a couple of years over it—really take their time, as if it was the most important thing they'd ever done—then it's difficult to stop seeing your own life through their eyes. Sometimes I'm nervous of my mind.'

She stood up with a brave flourish. 'Come on, strip off and let's get you washed. Then we'll have some food and I'll fuck you.'

Later, after Maitland had been washed by the girl, he lay on the bed in her towelling dressing gown. He felt fresh and revived. He had stood naked in the stair well as Jane worked away at his legs and abdomen with her strong hands, rubbing at the bruises and oil stains. As she prepared a small meal he watched her moving around the room, happy in this domestic retreat. She took out her smoker's kit and rolled a cigarette for herself.

'Jane, you smoke too much pot.'

'It's good for sex . . .'

She began to inhale the smoke. By the time they had finished their meal the room was filled with the fumes, and Maitland felt himself relax for the first time since his arrival on the island. She took off her skirt and lay on the bed beside him, propping her head next to his on the pillow. She offered him the loosely wrapped cigarette, but Maitland was already pleasantly high.

'That's nice . . .' She inhaled deeply on the smoke, and held his hand. 'How do you feel?'

'A lot better. It may sound strange, but for once I'm not all that keen to get away from here . . . Jane, where do you go to at night?'

'I work in a club—a kind of club, let's say. Now and then I pick someone up on the motorway. So what? Sordid, isn't it?'

'A little. Why don't you straighten your life out and make a start with someone?'

'Oh, come on . . . why don't you straighten your life out? You've got a hundred times more hang-ups. Your wife, this woman doctor—you were on an island long before you crashed here.'

She turned to face him. 'Well, Mr Maitland, I suppose I'd better undress—I don't think you could manage that job.'

Maitland lay passively with his hand on her hip. As she undressed, her mood underwent a curious change. Her jaunty smile faded. The awareness of her naked body seemed to distance her from Maitland, as if some defensive reflex was coming into play. She knelt across him, her sharp knees pressing into his chest wall. Maitland reached up to reassure her, but she pulled away, snapping in a hard voice.

'Not like this. First, I want some money. Come on, money for sex.'

'Jane . . . for God's sake.'

'Never mind God—I'm not fucking you for his sake or anyone else's.' She handed him his wallet. 'Five pounds—I want five pounds.'

'Jane, take it all. You can have it all.'

'Five!' She gripped his shoulders in her hands, nails tearing at his bruised skin. 'Come on—I can get ten on the motorway any night of the week!'

'Jane, your face—it's . . .'

'Never mind my face!'

Confused by this outburst, Maitland fumbled with the wallet. As he counted out the pound notes she tore them from his hand and stuffed them under the pillow.

Maitland held her breasts as she settled herself astride him. He tried to remember every pressure and movement of this sexual act, the orgasm that bolted through every over-stressed nerve in his body. He accepted the rules of the young woman's charade, glad of the freedom it implied, a recognition of their need to avoid any hint of commitment to each other. His relationships with Catherine and his mother, even with Helen Fairfax, all the thousand and one emotionally loaded transactions of his childhood, would have been tolerable if he had been able to pay for them in some neutral currency, hard cash across the high-priced counters of these relationships. Far from wanting this girl to help him escape from the island, he was using her for motives he had never before accepted, his need to be freed from his past, from his childhood, his wife and friends, with all their affections and demands, and to rove for ever within the empty city of his own mind.

Yet, at the end of their brief sexual act, Jane Sheppard reached under the pillow and drew out the five pound notes. She settled her hair, wincing at the cramp in her thighs. When Maitland hesitated, she took the notes from his hand and packed them back into his wallet.

19

beast and rider

'Wait, Proctor! Stop here!'

From his vantage point on Proctor's back, Maitland gazed across the central valley of the island. In the course of their afternoon patrol they had reached the abandoned churchyard to the south of the breaker's yard. Maitland could see along the entire length of the island, from the wire-mesh fence below the overpass to the western apex. The concrete junction of the two motorway routes shone in the sunlight like an elegant sculpture, and Maitland often visualized using its high deck as a pleasant roof garden.

Below him, Proctor leaned patiently against a tilting gravestone. One arm was clasped around Maitland's uninjured leg, holding the crippled man on his broad back. His creased face pressed against the worn letters of the nineteenth-century inscription. Maitland noticed him surreptitiously touching the letters with his scarred lips. The odour of Proctor's sweet sweat rose through the still air, like that of a well-groomed domestic animal. With his left hand Maitland held the collar of Proctor's dinner jacket. In his right he clasped the metal crutch, raising it to point out to himself the various features of the island that took his attention. By tapping Proctor with the straight end he was able to steer him around the island.

After glancing briefly at the afternoon traffic—an intermittent stream of cars, airline coaches and fuel tankers—Maitland turned his gaze westward again. He visited this observation post several times each day. From here he could see if any intruders had arrived on the island. In addition, he had so far failed to identify Jane Sheppard's escape route—somewhere along the embankment of the feeder road was a well-worn pathway.

'All right, Proctor—carry on. Take the short cut back to the Jaguar. For God's sake, don't drop me. I don't want to break the other damned leg.'

Proctor grunted noisily and wound himself up. Steadying Maitland on his back, he searched the deep grass in front of him, finding the worn churchyard steps that led to the former roadway below. As they moved through the grass Proctor steered himself with his scarred hand, his thick sensitive fingers feeling the density, moisture and inclination of the stems, rejecting one and selecting another of the well-used corridors.

'Proctor, I said the short cut.' Maitland tapped the tramp's head with the crutch, indicating a pathway that led over a steep hillock. Proctor ignored the command. This short cut, as he well knew, might expose Maitland too clearly to the passing traffic. Instead, he set off on a longer winding route well-screened by nettle banks and ruined walls.

Maitland submitted to this detour without argument. He had tamed the old tramp, but there was a tacit convention between them that Proctor would never help him to escape. He swayed from side to side on the tramp's back, balancing himself with the crutch like a tightrope walker. His right leg, as useless as the scabbard of a broken lance, trailed behind them.

Wheezing heavily, Proctor laboured towards the breaker's yard. Without this beast of burden Maitland found it difficult to move around the island at all. The grass and nettles, the elders and scruffy undergrowth had risen everywhere in the heavy rain that had drowned out the six days since his confrontation with Proctor. Although his injured thigh had begun to heal, Maitland was now much weaker. The combination of intermittent fever and contaminated food had reduced his weight by more than twenty pounds, and Proctor was able to carry his once large body without difficulty. Maitland could feel the bones of his thighs and pelvis emerging through his musculature—his skeleton come to greet him. Shaving himself in Jane Sheppard's travelling mirror, he would press and knead his cheeks and jaw. The bones were re-assembling themselves into a small, sharp face from which a pair of tired but fierce eyes stared out.

Despite his weakening physique, Maitland felt confident and clearheaded. With the end of the rain he could now get back to the task of planning his escape. He had passed the last two days of cold, torrential downpour sitting by himself over the paraffin stove in the basement room, well aware that he would be unable to climb the slopes of streaming mud.

Maitland looked up at the drying embankment. After two days of isolation, waiting for Jane Sheppard to reappear—she had finally returned that morning—a thin but distinct mental screen divided him from the traffic moving past. With a deliberate effort he thought of his wife, his son and Helen Fairfax, framing their faces in his mind. But they had become more and more remote, receding like the distant clouds over White City.

He clung to Proctor's back as they reached the breaker's yard. Grunting to himself, Proctor picked his way among the tyres lying about in the grass. Maitland realized that his confrontation with Proctor and Jane Sheppard had taken place at the latest possible moment. After a week of illness and semi-starvation he would now be unable to stand up to them.

'Right—put me down here. Careful . . . !'

Maitland tapped Proctor on the head with the crutch. Small-minded though it seemed, in some way he enjoyed reproving the tramp. He added a second blow, aiming the crutch at the thread of silver scar tissue running down Proctor's neck. He deliberately kept up his anger and testiness, encouraging himself to relish these punishments. Once he relaxed he would be destroyed by Proctor.

Proctor lifted his large, bowed back, easing Maitland on to the ground beside the Jaguar. He watched Maitland deferentially, but his dim tramp's eyes were alert for any false move. Maitland settled the crutch under his right arm. Supporting himself with one hand on Proctor's head, he moved stiffly towards the rear of the crashed car. The Jaguar was now hidden by the grass that had grown around it, covering all traces of the blackened ground.

Maitland avoided Proctor's eyes, composing his face so that it would show no trace of any expression. His one hope was that someone had come to inspect the car, a highway official or maintenance worker who might hand the licence number to an alert policeman.

Maitland peered into the grimy interior of the car, at the burnt-out front seat and instrument panel. No one had disturbed the tags of oily towelling and the empty bottles. Maitland gripped the roof gutter, forcing his palm against the sharp edge in an effort to rally himself.

To his surprise, he found that he was far stronger than he had thought. For several seconds he supported himself upright without the crutch. His right leg, though stiff at the hip joint, carried his weight, and by pivoting on his left leg he could very nearly walk. He decided to disguise the extent of his recovery. It would better serve his purpose if Jane and Proctor believed him to be a cripple.

'All right—let's see what we've got for you.'

Maitland beckoned Proctor out of his way, and opened the trunk. Proctor gazed at him with his crafty, expectant eyes, almost as if he were patiently waiting for Maitland to make a mistake. At times he seemed to invite Maitland to beat him with the crutch, as if well aware of Maitland's calculated pleasure in punishing him, urging him on in the hope that Maitland might develop a genuine taste and so never wish to leave the island.

Only the few gifts purchased by the young woman—a sliced loaf, a can of pressed pork bought at the neighbourhood supermarket—kept Proctor in check. Above all, several bottles of cheap red wine had maintained Maitland's authority. Proctor both feared and demanded this wine—in the evenings, when he had carried Maitland to the young woman's basement room, swept the floor and lit the lamp, he would return wearing his dinner jacket. Maitland would reward him with a cupful of the heady brew, and hand him the bottle. Proctor then retired to his den, where he would be drunk within minutes. As Maitland lay beside the young woman, smoking a cigarette with her before her regular departure for work in the evening, they would hear Proctor's trumpeting voice carried across the whispering grass, his deep mole-like music answered by the soft plaints of this green harp.

Proctor waited expectantly as Maitland lifted the lid. The trunk had been a cornucopia of extraordinary bounty for Proctor—a pair of heavy rubber overshoes, a set of imitation jade cufflinks Maitland had bought in Paris after mislaying his own, an old copy of *Life* magazine—each of these Proctor had taken off with him as if carrying away a priceless and mysterious treasure. Watching him, Maitland was convinced that Proctor had never been given anything in his life, and that his power over the tramp depended as much on the act of giving as on the evening bottles of wine. Perhaps one day they would dispense with the present itself and retain the act alone, devise an artificial currency of gesture and attitude.

Maitland stared into the trunk. Little remained apart from the car's tool kit, a gift he was reluctant to make. The tools might still prove useful in an escape.

'It looks as if there's nothing left, Proctor. A wheel brace won't be much use to you.'

Proctor gestured thickly, his face a planet of creases. Like a hungry child unable to accept the reality of a bare cupboard, he was working himself up to a climax of expectation. His face moved through a conflict of expressions—greed, patience, need. Hopping from one foot to the other, he jostled against Maitland, and nudged him in a not altogether friendly way.

Disturbed by this display, an ironic revenge on his own kindness towards the tramp—how much more docile Proctor became with a stick beating his neck—Maitland reached into the cardboard wine carton. Two bottles of the white Burgundy remained. He had intended to keep them both for himself, using Jane to buy the cheap Spanish claret for the tramp.

'All right, Proctor. You can have one of these. But don't drink it till this evening.'

He handed the bottle to the tramp, who seized it tightly, arms shaking with excitement. For a moment he seemed to be unaware of Maitland and the crashed car.

Maitland watched him quietly, fingering the crutch.

'You need me to ration it for you, Proctor—don't forget that. I've changed the whole economy of your life. Wine with your meals, you dress for dinner—you're all too eager to be exploited . . .'

As he rode back to the air-raid shelter, Maitland looked up at the high causeway of the overpass. After the days of rain the concrete had soon dried out, and the white flank crossed the sky like the wall of some immense aerial palace. Below the span were the approach roads to the Westway interchange, a labyrinth of ascent ramps and feeder lanes. Maitland felt himself alone on an alien planet abandoned by its inhabitants, a race of motorway builders who had long since vanished but had bequeathed to him this concrete wilderness.

'Free to go now . . .' he murmured to himself. 'Free to go . . .'

Resting in the sun, he sat against the wall of the air-raid shelter, the yellow shawl wrapped around him. Proctor squatted on the ground a few feet away, preparing to open his bottle of Burgundy. First, he went through a brief but careful ritual, which he performed with all the meat cans and biscuit packs that Maitland gave him. He scraped the label from the bottle with his knife and tore the fading paper into shreds. After giving the tramp the three-year-old copy of *Life* which he had found in the trunk of the Jaguar, hoping that the large photographs might turn Proctor's mind to the world beyond the island, Maitland had seen the magazine transformed into a pile of minutely ground confetti.

'You don't like words, do you, Proctor? You're even forgetting how to speak.'

The same was true of Proctor's sight. He was not going blind, Maitland was convinced, but simply preferred to rely on his scarred fingers and his sense of touch within the secure realm of the island's undergrowth.

Maitland turned towards the caisson of the feeder road, with its white concrete surface on which he had written his confused messages.

He snapped his fingers, charged with the sudden conviction that he would soon escape. Lifting the crutch like a schoolmaster, he pointed it at Proctor.

'Proctor, I'm going to teach you to read and write.'

the naming of the island

As he sat on the damp ground beside the caisson, Maitland watched Proctor working away like a happy child at the concrete surface. Within half an hour the reluctant pupil had become an eager apprentice. Already the wavering letters of his first alphabet had become strong and well-formed. Using both hands, he struck at the concrete slope, slashing his A's and X's side by side.

'Good, Proctor, you've learned quickly,' Maitland congratulated him. He felt a surge of pride in the tramp's achievement, the same pleasure he had found in teaching his son to play chess. 'It's a great invention—why don't we all write with both hands at once?'

Proctor gazed delightedly at his work. Maitland handed him two more of the cosmetic crayons he had taken from Jane Sheppard's room. Proctor held Maitland's arm, as if to reassure him of his seriousness as a pupil. To begin with, when Maitland had chalked up the first few letters of the alphabet, the tramp had refused even to look at them, cringing away as if they threatened some terrifying curse. After ten minutes of persuasion he had overcome his fear, and the lower surface of the caisson was covered with streaky letters.

Maitland pulled himself alongside Proctor. 'It doesn't take long, does it—all these years you've wasted . . . Now, let me show you how to write a few words. What do you want me to start with—circus, acrobat?'

Proctor's lips moved noiselessly. Shyly, he stuttered, 'P . . . P . . . Proct-or . . .'

'Your own name? Of course, I didn't think. It's a unique moment.' Maitland patted him on the back. 'Now watch. I want you to copy these in letters three feet high.'

He took the crayon from Proctor and wrote:

MAITLAND HELP

'P . . . P . . . Proctor . . .' he repeated, moving his fingers along the letters. 'That's your name. Now copy it in really large letters. Remember, it's the first time you've written your name.'

Eyes watering with pride, the tramp stared at the letters Maitland had chalked up, as if trying to engrave them for ever on his fading mind. He began to scrawl the letters across the concrete with both hands. Each word he started in its centre, moving outwards to left and right.

'Again, Proctor!' Maitland shouted above the roar of a truck climbing the feeder road. In his excitement the tramp was garbling the letters together into an indecipherable mass. 'Start again!'

Carried away by his own enthusiasm, Proctor ignored him. He scribbled away at the concrete, mixing up the fragments of Maitland's name, happily chalking the letters in streamers down to the ground, as if determined to cover every square inch of the island's surface with what he assumed to be his name.

Satisfied at last, he tottered away from the wall and sat down beside Maitland, beaming up at his handiwork.

'God Almighty . . .' Maitland leaned his head wearily against the crutch. The ruse had failed, partly because he had not taken into account Proctor's blubbery gratitude.

'Very good, Proctor—I'll teach you some more words.' When the tramp finally settled down Maitland leaned forward, whispering with deliberate archness, 'New words, Proctor—like "fuck" and "shit". You'd like to be able to write those. Wouldn't you?'

As Proctor tittered nervously Maitland wrote carefully:

HELP CRASH POLICE

He watched while Proctor reluctantly transcribed the words. He worked with only one hand, using the other to cover the letters he had written, as if frightened that he might be caught. He soon broke off, and rubbed away the message with the back of his hand, spitting on the coloured concrete.

'Proctor!' Maitland tried to stop him. 'No one will see you!'

Proctor threw the crayons on to the ground. He glanced with continuing pride at the straggling fragments of Maitland's name, and sat down in the grass. Maitland realized that Proctor had been only briefly amused by writing the obscene words on the wall, and was refusing to take part any further in what he considered to be a childish exhibition.

21

delirium

Exhausted now, his will fading, Maitland clung to Proctor's shoulders as they moved back and forth across the island. Bent beast and pale rider, they wandered through the seething grass. At intervals Maitland recovered and sat up, clutching the metal crutch. Trying to keep himself awake, he berated and beat Proctor at the slightest stumble or hesitation. The tramp laboured on, as if this pointless travel around the island was all that he could think of in his efforts to revive the injured man. At times he deliberately exposed the now inflamed scar on his neck, offering it to Maitland in the hope that abusing it would revive him.

On their third transit of the island, when they once again had reached the breaker's yard, Proctor lowered him to the ground. Maitland subsided weakly in the grass. The tramp lifted him in his powerful hands and placed him against the rear fender of the Jaguar. He shook Maitland's shoulders, trying to find the focus of his concentration.

Maitland turned his head away from the traffic. Refracted

through the afternoon heat, the motorways seemed to veer and loom, reverberating to the noise of the tyres and engines. He watched Proctor wandering around the breaker's yard, taking the rattraps from his belt and setting them among the wrecked cars. In the dusty roof of the overturned taxi Proctor traced with his finger the garbled fragments of Maitland's name.

When he saw Maitland looking at him he began to practise his gymnastics, hoping that a successful handstand or forward roll would restore Maitland's alertness. Maitland waited patiently as Proctor stumbled about, nervously wiping his nose each time he picked himself up. The warm air moved across the island, soothing both the grass and his own skin, as if these were elements of the same body. He remembered his attempt to shuck off portions of his own flesh, leaving those wounds at the places where they had been inflicted. His injured thigh and hip, his mouth and right temple, had all now healed, as if this magical therapy had somehow worked and he had successfully left these wounded members at their designated points.

In the same way, he was at last beginning to shed sections of his mind, shucking off those memories of pain, hunger and humiliation—of the embankment where he had stood screaming like a child for his wife, of the rear seat of the Jaguar, where he had inundated himself with self-pity . . . All these he would bequeath to the island.

Reviving at this prospect, he signalled to Proctor that he would mount his back. As they crossed the island, passing the churchyard again, Maitland saw that Proctor had been chalking fragments of his name on the ruined walls and headstones, on the rusting sheets of galvanized iron by the basement printshop. These cryptic anagrams, Proctor's serene message to himself, surrounded them everywhere.

Maitland scanned the perimeter of the island, hoping for any sign of the young woman. Her secret route to and from the island was his principal hope of escape. He waited for her to appear. Hungry, but unable to eat, he sat on the embankment by the wire-mesh fence as Proctor scavenged through the wire, selecting his morsels of ravaged food from the week-old dump. Maitland realized that he had forgotten what day it was—Wednesday, or perhaps Friday.

Proctor pressed the mess-tin towards him, offering a slice of wet bread covered with pieces of pork gristle. He was plainly worried by Maitland's barely coherent schemes to escape from the island.

Maitland thumped the ground with the crutch, waving the food away. From his wallet he removed a pound note and the stub of blue mascara pencil he had taken from Jane Sheppard's cosmetic table. 'We can buy food, Proctor—then we won't have to depend on *her* . . . For a pound we can—' He broke off with a thin shout, laughing to himself. 'God, you prefer these slops!'

He scribbled a brief rescue message in the margin of the note. He folded it and passed it to Proctor. 'We can have real food now, Proctor.'

Proctor took the note and pressed it gently into Maitland's hand.

Maitland lay back against the embankment, listening to the murmur of the afternoon traffic. Already the sun was beginning to fall in the western sky. The light flashed off the windshields of the first cars leaving the city in the rush hour.

A cooler wind moved below the overpass, stirring at the tags of refuse. Maitland opened his wallet and took out the bundle of pound notes. As Proctor stared at the money like a mesmerized animal Maitland placed the thirty banknotes in a series of rows, like a cardsharp laying out his last hand. He weighed each one down with a pebble.

'Wait, Proctor . . .' Maitland lifted one of the pebbles at random. The wind caught the note and whisked it away, carrying it across the island. Climbing into the air, the note swirled over the passing traffic, dived down and vanished under the wheels.

'Fly away, Peter . . .'

He lifted another pebble.

'Fly away, Paul . . .'

Proctor scuttled forward, trying to catch the second note, but it whirled away on the air. He clambered around Maitland like a nervous dog, trying to see what was wrong.

'Mr Maitland . . . please . . . no more flying money.'

'Flying money? Yes!' Maitland pointed to the tunnel of the overpass. 'There's more up there, Proctor, much more.' Aware that Proctor's attention was fixed on the rows of banknotes fluttering in the afternoon air, Maitland gathered them up. 'I was delivering a wages satchel. How much do you think was in it? Twenty thousand pounds! It's somewhere up there, Proctor. Did you see it in the tunnel when you straightened the barricade?' Maitland paused as the blunted templates of Proctor's mind locked into place. 'Listen, Proctor, you can have half. Ten thousand pounds. You'll be able to *buy* this island . . .'

He sat back, exhausted, as the tramp climbed eagerly to his feet, eyes wild with the promise of undreamt hopes.

As Proctor made his way across to the embankment, Maitland waited impatiently on the roof of the air raid shelter. Rattling the crutch, he watched the rush-hour traffic emerging from the overpass tunnel. His one remaining hope was that Proctor would enter the tunnel, be knocked down and killed. Only then would the traffic stop.

Proctor stood in the deep grass at the foot of the embankment. He looked back at Maitland, who waved him on. 'Go on, Proctor!' he shouted hoarsely. 'Buy the island!' To himself, he prayed aloud, 'Run him over . . .'

Barely able to control himself, he watched Proctor climb the embankment. The traffic was moving swiftly towards the tunnel from the Westway interchange.

'What is it?' Proctor had stepped on to the hard shoulder and was crouching behind the wooden palisade. He gazed back uncertainly in Maitland's direction, hands searching the unfamiliar air as the traffic roared past three feet above him.

With a scream of anger, Maitland clambered to his feet. Waving the crutch in the air over his head, he hobbled across the stony ground towards the embankment.

But Proctor had turned back. Ducking his head, he slid crabwise down the earth slope, his scarred hands reaching for the welcoming grass.

Maitland tottered forward, thrashing at the nettles with the crutch. As he slipped to the ground in frustration, Proctor came across the island to him. His large face appeared through the undergrowth like a worried but amiable beast's.

Maitland lay in the grass. He raised the crutch to strike at Proctor's legs. 'Go back . . . get the money!'

Proctor ignored the raised pipe, and extended his hand with a reassuring smile. Maitland looked up at him, realizing Proctor's reasons for coming back. In his muddled mind the tramp had assumed that if he found the money Maitland would leave the island, and so he had come back to care for him.

Gently he lifted Maitland on to his broad back.

'Proctor . . .' Maitland lolled unsteadily on his mount. '. . . you're waiting for me to die.'

Numbly he clung to the back of the tramp, his legs swaying against the rustling grass. The sweet scent of Proctor's body rose about him, for some reason identified in his mind with the smell of food. He was aware of Proctor carrying him into the deep under-world of grass and nettle-castles beside the churchyard. When the door of the crypt was unlocked he peered over Proctor's head into the dim chamber.

On one of the empty coffin shelves was a collection of metal objects stripped from his car, a wing mirror and manufacturer's medallion, strips of chromium trim, laid out like an elaborate altarpiece on which would one day repose the bones of a revered saint. Around them were the cuff links and overshoes that he had given to Proctor, a bottle of aftershave lotion and aerosol of shaving cream, the trinkets with which Proctor would dress his corpse.

22

the pavilion of doors

'Wake up! Are you all right?'

The grass seethed around him, the harsh stems whipping at his face. Maitland lay back in the late afternoon light, his arms outstretched, feeling the sunlight warm the bones of his chest. The yellow light moved across the grass, as if covering the blades with ever thicker layers of lacquer.

'Wake *up!*' The young woman's shrill voice roused him. She knelt in the deep grass and touched his shoulder, her eyes peering down suspiciously.

'Listen, are you feeling okay?' She looked over her shoulder at Proctor, crouching uneasily by the entrance to the cinema basement. 'Proctor, what the hell have you been doing to him? I don't know—maybe we ought to stick him up on the road somewhere and let the police find him.'

'*No!*'

Maitland stretched out a claw-like hand. He held Jane's right arm in a fierce grip. 'No—I want to stay here. For the time being.'

'All right . . .' The girl rubbed a bruised nerve. 'Stay here. I warn you, though, I might decide to leave. You can have my room.'

Maitland shook his head, trying to calm the girl. His sleep had refreshed him, and he felt calm and clearheaded again. He remembered the endless journeys on Proctor's back across the island, and the multiplying fragments of his own name that had seemed to taunt and confuse him. Perhaps the fever had returned without him realizing it, or hunger had made him light-headed enough to try to kill Proctor. As for the young woman, she was spending less and less time on the island—he would have to think up some way of keeping her there.

'Jane, if you go, I'll die here. Proctor's already planning to bury me.'

The young woman's eyes were like those of a pensive child examining an unfamiliar creature. 'But your leg looks better to me. You were nearly walking this morning.' She stood up, shaking her head. 'I don't know. All right, I'll stay. I brought the wine. I'll give it to Proctor.'

'Not yet.' Maitland sat up, his mind alert. He pointed a hand at Proctor. 'I want him to bring his bed.'

'Where to? He's not going to sleep with us.'

'Here. Ask him to bring it here. And then I want him to build a shelter for me. I'll tell him how to do it.'

Two hours later, Maitland lay back in the small shack, a pavilion of rust, which Proctor had built around him out of the discarded sections of car bodies. A semicircle of doors formed the sides, tied together by their window pillars. Above, two hoods completed a primitive roof. Maitland lay comfortably in the open doorway of the pavilion, watching with satisfaction as Proctor completed the last assembly. He had brought not only his bed for Maitland, but two patched quilts. He lifted Maitland on to the bed and arranged the quilts around him. Fragments of the tramp's finger writing covered several of the door panels, but Maitland decided to let these stay.

'He's done a good job.' Jane had sauntered around the pavilion as Proctor laboured back and forth. Smoking the cigarette she had rolled, she kept half an eye on the distant traffic. Maitland's shack was shielded from the motorway by the high grass and ruined out-buildings. 'At least as good as most of the speculative building that's going up these days. I can see that you're a real architect.'

She leaned against a door, talking to Maitland through a window after winding down the glass. 'Are you going to spend the night here?'

'No—this is my—summer house.'

'What about his wine? Shall I give it to him?'

Proctor was squatting patiently nearby, wiping the sweat off his face with an old towel. He held the dinner jacket in his hands, as if nervous of putting it on in case this aroused Maitland's irritation. His eyes were fixed on the bottle of wine in Jane's hands. Maitland pointed to the derelict paybox.

'Tell him to wait over there. Where I can't see him.'

'He's worked hard for you.'

'Jane . . .' Wearily, Maitland beckoned her away. His emaciated body was lit by the red light of the setting sun. 'I'm not concerned with him any more.'

He took the bottle from her and raised it to his lips. He drank steadily, barely tasting the harsh wine. Like a mendicant desert chief presiding over his barren kingdom, he squatted on the bed in the mouth of the rusty pavilion. He had now gone beyond exhaustion and hunger to a state where the laws of physiology, the body's economy of needs and responses, had been suspended. He listened to the traffic, his eye on the red disc of the sun sinking behind the apartment blocks. The glass curtain wall was jewelled by the light. The roar of the traffic seemed to come from the sun.

Maitland sat forward, handing the wine to Jane Sheppard as he stared hard at the apex of the island. For a brief moment he had seen the familiar white-haired figure of the old man with the light motorcycle, moving along the eastbound carriageway. His white hair had been bathed by the setting sun as he and his machine had appeared in a gap between two streams of traffic. Maitland tried to find him again, but gave up as vehicles clogged all lanes of the motorway. He remembered his previous state of terror on first seeing the old man. This time, by contrast, he felt reassured.

'Proctor's still waiting for his wine.'

The young woman stood in front of him, swaying aggressively, one hand holding the bottle by its neck. Most of the wine had gone, and Maitland realized that she had been drinking beside him for at least ten minutes. In her ugly euphoria, his silence only provoked her.

'You're a shit. Are you dying? Don't die here.'

Maitland watched her as she smoked her cigarette. She tossed her hair with a flourish, challenging Maitland's fascination with the sinking sun.

'You think you're going to leave here. Let me tell you, you're not. You imagine you can just lie here, thinking all day. No one gives a damn what you think. You—you're no one.'

Maitland drifted away from her, dimly aware of her voice drumming through the darkening air. He was convinced that his body
was no longer absorbing anything he ate or drank—the wine formed
a cold lake within his stomach.

The girl struck his face with her hand, trying to hold his
attention.

'Who are you going to hate next?' she asked aggressively. 'Aren't
you being a little selective? You humiliate me with this kind of conversation. Take my word, I know more about beds than you do. I
think you're a lousy middle-aged creep and I'm not going to pay your
fucking bill. God—lunatic man you are. You're demented.'

Maitland turned his head, following her as she stalked up and
down outside the pavilion, ranting to herself. She swayed about to
some music in her head, and he knew that she was talking to
someone else.

'I'm not dancing around this flat, I'm shuffling. It doesn't matter,
it's so good. Let's keep our cool and we'll be separated by tomorrow afternoon. It's beautiful music, actually. Listen, I don't need
anyone to like me. I'm past it. Don't be a child. How great that you
and I are finished. I never want to see you again. I regard our relationship as ended. Please do not ring me on the telephone. Please
do not interfere with my professional relationships. This is a beautiful record. It's great for sexual intercourse. You ought to try it
sometime.'

In a moment of lucidity she stared down at Maitland through
the reddening light, recognizing him before anger clouded her mind
again.

'You'll get yourself run over, baby. Thank God you'll soon be out
of my life. You ought to live in an oriental bazaar. I loved you dearly

and you buggered it up. Just twelve hours and you'll be gone. Who wants relationships? You bore me right now. You never had any love and affection as a child. Don't commit any acts of violence tonight. There are lots of nice children here. Why are you such a shit? That fucking American girl. She's a whore. So conceptual. She's so brilliant. I know . . .'

Her voice ended. She fumbled on the ground for the wine bottle she had dropped, picked it up and threw it with a cry at Proctor, who was crouching in the fading light beside the paybox. The bottle smashed against the wooden shutters. The glass fragments gleamed like crazed eyes.

Proctor moved from one fragment to the next, licking the pieces with his scarred lips. Maitland listened passively to the young woman when she began to taunt him with her promiscuity, almost as if she believed that he was the father of her dead child.

Maitland stood up and stepped over to her. Holding off her strong arms, he pulled her shoulders against his chest. He soothed and comforted her, brushing the wet hair from her face. When she had calmed, he steered her towards the entrance to the basement.

They sat on the bed together in the warm room. She choked briefly into her hands, her eyes clearing. Reviving, she turned urgently to Maitland.

'Look, you mustn't stay here any longer. You're a bag of bones. Your mind—you need a doctor. I'll telephone your wife right now, they'll come and get you this evening . . .'

'No.' Calmly, Maitland took her hands. 'Don't call her. Do you understand?'

'All right.' She nodded reluctantly. 'Listen, rest in here tonight.

I'll help you on to the road tomorrow. We'll take you to a hospital.'

'Fine, Jane. We'll stay together.' Maitland put his arm around her shoulders. 'I don't want anyone to know I'm on the island.'

She leaned wearily against his chest.

'Proctor wants to leave. He asked me to take him with me.'

23

the trapeze

Shortly after dawn, the first sunlight shone on to the traffic island through the concrete pillars of the overpass. Leaning on the metal crutch, Maitland moved down the central valley. As he swung himself along the uneven ground he searched the high embankments with the sharp eyes of a gamekeeper on the lookout for an escaping poacher.

For an hour he had been patrolling the island, and the dew from the grass soaked his ragged trousers. As the last of the all-night trucks laboured along the motorway he rested outside the bolted door of Proctor's shelter. He looked up at the complex shadows and geometries formed by the route signs and overhead wires, lamp standards and concrete walls. A solitary car moved along the westbound carriageway, and Maitland raised the crutch and waved to it. Despite all his disappointments during his long struggle to escape from the island, he still clung to the hope that a passing driver would suddenly stop for him.

Maitland left the shelter and swung himself towards the

sunlight emerging below the overpass. Fifty yards from the wire-mesh fence he let out a gasp of surprise, dropping the crutch into the damp grass.

A municipal repair vehicle was parked in the centre of the deserted span. Only the roof of the driver's cab and the telescopic platform were visible above the concrete balustrade, but Maitland could see that workmen would soon be climbing over the side to repair the underside of the span, where sections of the cement were flaking away. A workman's cradle hung from the balustrade. Ropes trailed over the edge, one coil reaching to within six feet of the ground.

Confused by the sight of the vehicle, Maitland fumbled in the air for the crutch. He whispered hoarsely, a reflex cry for help. Their heads briefly visible above the balustrade, the driver and two workmen were walking towards a second repair vehicle parked three hundred yards along the road.

Shaking with excitement, Maitland picked up the crutch and swung himself forwards. Ten feet behind him, a black-suited figure darted from the deep grass. As Maitland turned, tripping over a rusty sheet of galvanized iron, he recognized Proctor. The tramp ran forward, arms outstretched above his head. Under the dinner jacket he wore the ragged leotard. Leaping over the discarded tyres in the grass, he ran towards the coil of rope hanging six feet from the ground.

'Proctor! Leave it!'

Maitland seized the crutch and lurched forward, beating the ground in an attempt to frighten Proctor away. But the old acrobat had already leapt into the air. He caught the loose coil, swung free and pulled himself upwards hand over hand. His powerful arms moved like pistons, his feet twisted around the loose end of the rope in a running hold.

Almost speechless with fear, Maitland struck at the swinging rope with the crutch. Once Proctor escaped, the young woman would soon abandon him. He was certain that her offer to call for help the previous evening had been no more than a ruse. The moment she reached the embankment she would have vanished, to be followed almost immediately by the tramp. Left alone on the island, Maitland would survive no more than a few days.

Proctor climbed on to the balustrade. Confirming Maitland's fears, he glanced down at him, a crafty grin on his face.

'Proctor! Come down!'

Lifting himself on his strong hands, Proctor swung his legs over the balustrade. He scanned the empty roadway. With a wave to Maitland, he unwound the ropes holding the workman's cradle and lowered the wooden platform on its steel frame. He seized the guy ropes attached to the winch on the repair truck, sidestepped over the balustrade and leapt on to the cradle.

As Proctor lowered the cradle towards the ground Maitland realized that the tramp, far from trying to elude him, was in fact attempting to help Maitland escape. Still trying to impress Maitland with his expertise as a sometime trapeze artist, he swung the cradle from side to side.

'Great, Proctor . . .' Maitland muttered to himself. 'I'm very impressed. Now, come down.'

But Proctor was no longer aware of Maitland. Twenty feet above the ground, he swung the cradle in ever wider arcs. His powerful body radiated confidence in every movement. He tore off the dinner jacket and tossed it away towards the ground whirling below him. With an expert flip he jumped from the cradle at the top of its swing and caught the metal frame in his strong hands. Jackknifing his body, he propelled the cradle through the air. At the top of the next swing he swivelled in the air, reversed his hands and propelled the cradle back again. His creased face was transformed by a child-like smile.

A voice shouted from the road. The cab door slammed. A moment later the engine of the repair vehicle roared into life. Hanging from the swinging cradle, Proctor looked up uncertainly. Already the coils of rope attached to the winch were tightening, the loops racing around his shoulders. Maitland waved the crutch at the tramp, signalling him to jump. The repair vehicle was moving off, its driver unaware that Proctor was entangled in the loose lines attached to the winch.

The driver accelerated, changing his gears. Before Proctor could free himself he was jerked backwards off the cradle. The guy ropes ran around him, tightening across his waist and neck. Trussed like a carcass in an abattoir, he hung above the cradle. Legs kicking as he grappled with the ropes, he was carried backwards through the air.

The repair vehicle picked up speed, its engine drowning Maitland's shouts. Proctor hung helplessly as it moved above him, carrying him towards the nearest concrete pillar. When his body struck the pillar it thudded like a punchbag against the massive column. Unconscious now, he hung limply from the rope around his neck. He was carried through the air below the overpass, until the ropes became entangled in the angular frame of a route indicator.

There was a whiplike snap as the ropes parted. The repair vehicle carried on. Proctor's garotted body fell to the damp ground below.

24

escape

The rush-hour traffic moved along the motorway. The hard roar of engines drummed across the island. Shielded by the high grass, Maitland and Jane Sheppard sat beside Proctor's body. The roofs of the air-raid shelters rose around them like the backs of ancient animals buried asleep in the soil.

Proctor lay face upwards, his face and shoulder covered by a rose-pattern quilt which Jane had taken from his den. The light wind uncovered the upper corner of the quilt, revealing part of Proctor's face. Maitland leaned forward and replaced the worn cloth.

Jane wiped her hands on the grass, catching her breath after helping to drag the body across the island. She was still white-faced, the sharp bones of her cheeks and forehead like knives below the skin. She reached out and touched Maitland, as if uncertain of his response.

'I'm leaving now,' she said. 'The police will soon be here.'

Maitland nodded. 'Yes, you ought to leave now.'

'I'm not involved in this—it's between you and Proctor.'

'Of course.'

'What are you going to do with him?'

'Bury him—I'll find a shovel somewhere.'

Jane pushed at Maitland's shoulder, trying to wake him. 'Do you need any help? If you don't mind . . . funerals give me the shudders.'

'No . . .' Maitland's sunken eyes stared through the dirt on his face. 'Just leave me here.'

'What are you going to do? You can't stay.'

'Jane, I want to leave in my own way.'

She shrugged, getting to her feet. 'It's just that we talked about going together . . . suit yourself.' She gazed distastefully at Proctor. 'It was probably a heart attack. A pity—in his way he was good at acrobatics. What about food? I could bring some back for you.'

'That's all right. There is food here.'

'Where?' She followed his eyes to the wire-mesh fence. 'I don't think you should stay here any longer. I'll help you on to the embankment, we'll take a taxi.' When Maitland made no reply she pulled his shoulder. '*Listen!* I'll call for help! They'll be here in half an hour!'

In a clear voice, Maitland spoke to her for the last time. 'Jane, don't call for help. I'll leave the island, but I'll do it in my own time.' He took out his wallet and handed her the bundle of greasy notes. 'Take all these, I won't need them. But promise me you will tell no one I'm here.'

With a grimace of regret, she put away the money. She dusted her knees and walked through the air-raid shelters towards the cinema basement.

Ten minutes later she had gone. Maitland watched her climb the embankment of the feeder road. He realized that there was no secret pathway—she walked straight up the slope, picking her way along a succession of familiar footholds, the suitcase in a strong hand. She stepped over the crash barrier. Within a minute a car stopped for her, and she was carried away among the trucks and airline coaches.

After an hour, when the police had failed to appear, Maitland decided that she had kept her bargain. He picked up the shovel the girl had thrown at his feet before she left. Leaving the crutch, he crawled through the grass, feeling his way with his outstretched hands, sensing the stronger vibrations of the tall grass growing from the churchyard.

It was late morning by the time Maitland had completed the burial. Exhausted by the effort of dragging the tramp's body among the shelters, Maitland lay on the bed in his pavilion of doors, watching the traffic move along the motorway. He had buried Proctor in the floor of the crypt, surrounding the grave with the metal objects taken from the Jaguar, and the overshoes, aerosol can and other gifts which he had made the tramp.

Despite his exertion and the fact that he had taken little food, Maitland felt a sense of gathering physical strength, as if the unseen powers of his body had begun to discharge their long-stored energies. His leg had been by no means as badly injured as he had believed. There was even a slight movement in the hip joint, and he would soon be able to walk without the crutch. He was glad that both Proctor and the young woman had gone. Their presence had brought out unwelcome strains in his character, qualities irrelevant to the task of coming to terms with the island.

As well as this new-found physical confidence, Maitland noticed a mood of quiet exultation coming over him. He lay calmly in the doorway of his pavilion, realizing that he was truly alone on the island. He would stay there until he could escape by his own efforts. Maitland tore away the remains of his ragged shirt, and lay bare-chested in the warm air, the bright sunlight picking out the sticks of his ribs. In some ways the task he had set himself was meaningless. Already he felt no real need to leave the island, and this alone confirmed that he had established his dominion over it.

A police car moved along the motorway, the co-driver watching the deep grass. Secure in his pavilion, Maitland waited for it to pass. When it had gone he stood up and gazed confidently across the island. He felt light-headed from hunger, but calm and in control of himself. He would collect food from the perimeter fence—and, perhaps, as a gesture in the direction of the old tramp, leave a token portion beside his grave.

In a few hours it would be dusk. Maitland thought of Catherine and his son. He would be seeing them soon. When he had eaten it would be time to rest, and to plan his escape from the island.